BEFORE HE SINS

(A MACKENZIE WHITE MYSTERY—BOOK 7)

BLAKE PIERCE

ISBN: 978-1-64029-158-4

BOOKS BY BLAKE PIERCE

PROLOGUE

The sun had cracked the horizon but had not yet burned off the last chills of night—Christy's favorite time of day. Seeing the sun come up over the city was a stark reminder for her that every night had its end, something she needed to know, as she had started to feel further and further away from God. Seeing the sun coming up over the buildings of Washington, DC, and pushing away the night reminded her of the lyrics to a worship song: *Although there's pain in the night, the sun comes in the morning...*

She recited that line over and over as she walked up the street toward the church. She'd been trying to talk herself into doing this for weeks now. Her faith had been challenged, as she had given in to sin and temptation. The idea of confession had come to her right away but it was also hard. It was never easy to confess one's sins. But she knew she had to. The longer a sin existed between her and God, the harder it would be to correct that imbalance. The sooner she could confess that sin, the better chance she had of regaining her footing and reestablishing her faith—a faith that had defined her life ever since the age of ten.

As she saw the edges of the church come into view, her heart sagged. *Can I really do this? Can I really confess this?*

The familiar edges and shape of Blessed Heart Catholic Church seemed to tell her that yes, she could.

Christy started to tremble. She wasn't sure she'd call what she had been doing an affair or not. She'd only kissed the man once and had called it out for what it was then. But she had continued to see him, had continued to let herself be lifted up by his words of praise and adoration—words her own husband had stopped uttering to her years ago.

She could almost feel that sin burned away from her as the sun rose higher in the sky, casting golds and soft oranges around the edges of Blessed Heart. If she needed any further sign that she was supposed to be confessing her sins to a priest on this particular morning, that was it.

She came to the steps of Blessed Heart with a heaviness on her shoulders. But she knew that within moments, it would be gone.

1

She could return home, her sins confessed, her heart unburdened, and her mind—

When she reached the front doors, Christy screamed.

She backed away, still screaming. She nearly fell down the concrete stairs as she stumbled back. Her hands went to her mouth, doing very little to muffle the scream.

Father Costas was hanging from the doors. He had been stripped down to his underwear and there was a long horizontal cut on his brow. His head hung down, looking toward his bare feet, which were dangling two feet above the concrete stoop. Little tendrils of blood dripped from his toes, collecting in a dingy pool on the stoop.

Crucified, Christy thought. *Father Costas has been crucified.*

CHAPTER ONE

Following her last case, Mackenzie White had done something she had never once done before as a working woman: she had asked for a vacation.

She'd requested a two-week vacation for a number of reasons and within just a single day, she knew she had made the right decision. She'd wasted no time in bolstering her reputation when she had come to the FBI. By no design of her own, she had ended up handling high-profile cases that seemed to come looking for her. Not only that, but she had excelled at them and had impressed all of the right people in Quantico and DC. After successfully wrapping up numerous cases and putting her life on the line on a monthly basis, she thought two weeks of paid vacation wasn't too much to ask.

Her superiors had agreed—and even encouraged it. She was sure they'd get a kick out of knowing how she had been spending most of that time—in numerous gyms and workout facilities, getting her body into better shape, sharpening her instincts and skills. She had a solid base for all of the important things. She was adept at hand-to-hand combat. She was eerily good with a firearm. She was much stronger than most other women she had gone through the academy with.

But Mackenzie White was always wanting to improve upon herself.

That's why, eight days into her two-week vacation, she was working up a sweat and a multitude of sore muscles at a private gym. She was pushing herself away from the corner of one of several boxing rings, giving her sparring partner a nod of gratitude. She was stepping into a second practice round and was fully expecting to get defeated. And that was okay.

She'd only been practicing Muay Thai for a little over a month now. She had gotten good enough at it that she was comfortable introducing another, lesser known, fighting style with it. With the help of a private instructor and a hell of a lot of determination, Mackenzie had also started training in Yaw-Yan, a Filipino style of kickboxing. Mixing the two was rather unorthodox but she and her trainer had worked on a way to utilize them both. It pushed

Mackenzie physically, to the point where her shoulders and calves felt like slabs of brick.

She felt those muscles responding now as she stepped to her partner. They touched gloves and resumed their session. She immediately dodged a jab and countered with a low jab of her own.

It was, in a way, like learning a new style of dance. Mackenzie had taken part in dance classes as a girl and had never forgotten the importance of footwork and focus. They were disciplines she carried with her into her first job as a street cop, then into her job as a detective out in Nebraska. Those basic disciplines had also helped her immensely as an FBI agent, saving her life on more than one occasion.

They also came rushing back to her as she sparred. She tried out her new moves and instruction, using a series of downward kicks and elbow attacks combined with more traditional kickboxing attacks. She used the surprised expression of her sparring partner as fuel, motivating her. Sure, it was just practice, but she felt the need to excel there as well.

It also helped to clear her mind. She always associated each punch, kick, or elbow strike with something from her past. A left jab was directed at years of neglect with the Nebraska PD. A back-handed attack with her right swatted away the fear the Scarecrow Killer case had instilled in her. A pivot and jab was a blow to the heart of the endless stream of mysteries coming out of her father's old case.

If she was being honest with herself, it was that case that had pushed her to learn these new fighting disciplines—to make sure she continued to evolve as a fighter. She had received a note from someone involved...someone in the shadows who apparently knew who she was.

She still saw that note in her mind's eye as she sparred.

Stop looking...

Naturally, she intended to do just the opposite. And that's why she was currently in the ring, her gaze focused and her muscles as taut as violin strings.

When she landed a blow to her opponent's solar plexus and then a padded-elbow strike to her sparring partner's ribs, the session was called from the side of the ring. The judge was smiling and nodding as he softly applauded.

"Okay, Mac," he said. "Give it a break for a while, huh? You're at an hour and a half today."

Mackenzie nodded, dropping her stance and again tapping gloves with her sparring partner—a twenty-five-year-old male who

4

had the build of an MMA fighter. He gave her a quick grin over his mouthpiece and made a quick exit through the ropes.

Mackenzie thanked the judge and then headed for the locker rooms. Her muscles were sore to the point of trembling, but she enjoyed it. It meant she was pushing herself, stretching herself to new limits.

As she showered and slid into what Ellington referred to as her gym swag (an Under Armour tank top and a pair of black dry-fit leggings), she reminded herself that she had one more workout for the day. She hoped her arms were done trembling by then. Sure, Ellington would be there to help, but she had several rather heavy boxes to move around this afternoon.

While she had been technically living at Ellington's apartment for the past few days, today would be the day she actually moved things in. It was yet another of the many reasons she had asked for a two-week vacation. The thought of trying to move over the course of a weekend had not appealed to her. Plus, she figured, this was yet another way she was growing and evolving. Trusting someone else enough to share a living space and, as cheesy as it seemed, her heart, was something she had been incapable of until a few months ago.

And as soon as she was changed into her gym swag, she found that she could barely wait to start moving things in. Sore or not, she put a little extra speed in her step on the way to the parking lot.

***

The upside to not being a materialistic person was that when it came time to move, there was very little to pack up. As such, a single trip in Ellington's pickup truck and a rented U-Haul did the job. The move itself took less than two hours thanks to the elevator in Ellington's building, and in the end, she really didn't have to lift that many boxes.

They celebrated the move with Chinese food and a bottle of wine. Mackenzie was tired, sore, but immensely happy. She'd been expecting to feel nervous and maybe even a bit of regret over the move, but as they started unpacking boxes over their dinner, she found that she was excited for this next stage of her life.

"Here's the deal," Ellington said as he placed a box cutter to a stream of packing tape along the top of one of the boxes. "You need to tell me now if I'm going to find any overly embarrassing movies or CDs in these boxes."

"I think the most embarrassing CD you'll find is the soundtrack to that awful nineties remake of *Romeo and Juliet*. But what can I say? I really liked that Radiohead song."

"Then you're forgiven," he said, cutting into the tape.

"How about you?" she asked. "Any embarrassing media lying around?"

"Well, I got rid of all of my CDs and DVDs. Everything's digital. I needed to free up the space. It's almost as if I had a sneaking suspicion that this sexy FBI lady was going to be moving in with me one of these days."

"Good instincts," she said. She walked over to him and took his hands in hers. "Now…this is your last chance. You can back out now before we start taking things out of the boxes."

"Back out? Are you crazy?"

"You'll have a girl living with you," she said, pulling him close. "A girl that tends to like things neat. A girl that can get a little OCD."

"Oh, I know," he said. "I'm looking forward to it."

"Even all the ladies' clothes? You willing to share your closet?"

"I have very few clothes," he said, leaning in close to her. Their noses were almost touching and a heat that they had gotten used to was starting to build between them. "You can have all of the closet space you want."

"Makeup and tampons, sharing a bed, and another person dirtying up dishes. You sure you're ready for that?"

"Yeah. One question, though."

"What's that?" she said. Her hands traveled from his hands to his arms. She knew where this was going and every sore muscle in her body was ready.

"All of those ladies' clothes," he said, "You can't be leaving them on the floor all the time."

"Um, I don't intend to," she said.

"Oh, I know," he said. He then reached down and lifted the tank top off of her. He wasted no time in doing the same to the sports bra underneath. "But I probably will," he added, throwing both to the floor.

He kissed her then and although he tried leading her into the bedroom, their bodies did not have the patience. They ended up on the living room rug and although Mackenzie's sore muscles protested the hard floor under her back, other parts of her body overruled them.

When her phone rang at 4:47 in the morning, a single thought went through Mackenzie's sleepy mind as she reached for the bedside table.

A call at this hour…I guess my vacation is over.

"Yeah?" she asked, not bothering with formalities as she was technically on vacation.

"White?"

In an odd way, she had nearly missed McGrath over these last nine days. Still, hearing his voice was like a very quick and stark return to reality.

"Yes, I'm here."

"Sorry for the early call," he said. And before he added anything else, Mackenzie heard Ellington's phone ring from the other side of the bed.

Something big, she thought. *Something bad.*

"Look, I know I signed off on your two weeks," McGrath said. "But we've got a mess on our hands here and I need you on it. You and Ellington. Meet me in my office as soon as you can."

It wasn't a question, but a direct order. And without anything resembling a *goodbye,* McGrath killed the call. Mackenzie let out a sigh and looked over at Ellington, who was finishing up his own call.

"Well, looks like your vacation is over," he said with a thin smile.

"That's fine," she said. "It ended on quite a bang."

And then, like some old married couple, they kissed and slid out of bed, heading in to work.

CHAPTER TWO

The J. Edgar Hoover building was empty as Mackenzie and Ellington entered. They'd both been in its hallways at all hours of the night, so it was nothing out of the ordinary. Still, to be called in to work at such an hour was never a good thing. It usually meant there was something truly awful waiting for them.

When they reached McGrath's office, they found his door open. He was sitting at a small conference table in the back of his office, looking over a variety of files. There was another agent there with him, a woman Mackenzie had seen before. Her name was Agent Yardley, a quiet, no-bullshit type of woman who had stepped in to help Agent Harrison from time to time. She gave a nod and a robotic sort of smile when they entered the room and stepped up to the conference room table. She looked back at her laptop, focused on whatever was on the screen.

When McGrath looked up at Mackenzie, she couldn't help but notice what looked like slight relief in his eyes. It was a nice way to be introduced back into work after having her vacation cut short.

"White, Ellington," McGrath said. "You know Agent Yardley?"

"Yes," Mackenzie said, giving the agent a nod of acknowledgment.

"She's just come back from a crime scene that is linked to another we had five days ago. I originally had her on the case but when I thought we might have a serial on our hands, I asked her to provide everything she had so I could hand it off to you two. We've got a murder...the second of its kind in five days. White, I called you specifically because I want you on it based on your history—the Scarecrow Killer specifically."

"What's the case?" Mackenzie asked.

Yardley turned her laptop toward them. Mackenzie went to the chair closest to it and took a seat. She looked at the image on the screen with a deadened sort of quiet that she had come to know well—the ability to study a picture of something grotesque as part of her job but with a resigned sympathy most humans would feel at such a tragic death.

She saw an older man, his hair and beard mostly gray, hanging from the door of a church. His arms were extended and his head was bowed down in a show of mock crucifixion. There were slash marks on his chest and a large gash on his forehead. He had been stripped down to his underwear, which had caught a great deal of the blood that had drained down from his brow and chest. From what she could see in the pictures, she was pretty sure his hands had literally been nailed to the door. The feet, though, were simply tied together.

"This is the second victim," Yardley said. "Reverend Ned Tuttle, fifty-five years of age. He was discovered by an old woman who had stopped by the church early to put flowers on her husband's grave. Forensics is on the scene as we speak. It seems the body was put there less than four hours ago. We've already had agents speak with the family to notify them."

A woman who likes to take charge and get things done, Mackenzie thought. *Perhaps she and I would get along well together.*

"What do we have on the first victim?" Mackenzie asked.

McGrath slid her a folder. As she opened it up and looked over the contents, McGrath filled her in. "Father Costas, of the Blessed Heart Catholic Church. He was found in the same state, nailed to the doors of his church five days ago. I'm honestly quite surprised you didn't see anything about it on the news."

"I made a point not to watch the news on my vacation," she said, cutting McGrath a look that was meant to be comical but, she felt, went totally unacknowledged.

"I remember hearing about it around the water cooler," Ellington said. "The woman who discovered the body was in a state of shock for a while, right?"

"Right," McGrath said.

"And based on what forensics came up with," Yardley added, "Father Costas had certainly not been nailed there for any longer than two hours."

Mackenzie looked through the files. The images inside showed Father Costas in the exact same position as Reverend Tuttle. Everything looked pretty much identical, right down to the elongated gash across the brow.

She closed the file and slid it back over to McGrath.

"Where is this church?" Mackenzie asked, pointing back to the laptop screen.

"Just outside of town. A decent-sized Presbyterian church."

"Text me the directions," Mackenzie said, already getting to her feet. "I'd like to go see it for myself."

Apparently, she had missed working over the last eight days more than she had realized.

***

It was still dark when Mackenzie and Ellington arrived at the church. The forensics team was just finishing up their work. The body of Reverend Tuttle had been removed from the door but that was fine with Mackenzie. Based on the two images she had seen of Father Costas and Reverend Tuttle, she'd seen all she needed to see.

Two crucifixion-style murders, both on the front doors of churches. The men killed were the presumed leaders of those churches. It's pretty clear someone has a pretty big grudge against the church. And whoever they are, it's not specific to one particular denomination.

She and Ellington approached the front of the church as the forensics team wrapped things up. Off to the left, near the small plaque board with the church's name on it, was a small group of people. A few of them were in prayer while they embraced. Others were openly weeping.

Members of the church, Mackenzie assumed with a resounding sadness.

They neared the church and the scene only got worse. There were smears of blood and two large holes where the nails had been driven in. She looked the area over for any further religious iconography but saw nothing. There was just blood and bits of dirt and sweat.

Such a bold move, she thought. *There's got to be some sort of symbolism to it. Why a church? Why the doors of a church? Once would be a coincidence. But two in a row, both nailed to the doors—that's purposeful.*

She found it almost offensive that someone would do such a thing in front of a church. And maybe that was the point of it. There was no way to know for sure. While Mackenzie was not a strong believer in religion or God or the effects of faith, she also fully respected the rights of people who *did* live by faith. Sometimes she wished she was that kind of person. Maybe that was why she found this act so deplorable; mocking the death of Christ at the very entryway to a place where people gathered to seek solace and refuge in his name was detestable.

"Even if this was the first murder," Ellington said, "a sight like this would instantly make me think there were more coming. This is…revolting."

"It is," Mackenzie said. "But I can't be quite sure why it makes me feel that way."

"Because churches are safe places. You don't expect to see large nail holes and wet blood on their doors. That's some Old Testament shit right there."

Mackenzie wasn't anything close to a Biblical scholar but she did recall Bible stories from her childhood—something about the Angel of Death passing through a city and collecting the firstborns of every family if there was not a certain marking over their doors.

A chill crept through her. She repressed it by turning to the forensics team. With a slight wave, she got the attention of a member of their team. He came over, clearly a little distraught over what he and the rest of the team had seen. "Agent White," he said. "This your case now?"

"Seems like it. I was wondering if you guys still had the nails that were used to put him up there."

"Sure do," he said. He waved over another of his team members and then looked back to the door. "And the guy who did this…he was either strong as hell or had all the time in the world to do this."

"That's doubtful," Mackenzie said. She nodded back out toward the church parking lot and the street beyond. "Even if the killer did this around two or three in the morning, the chances of a vehicle not traveling down Browning Street and seeing him are slim to none."

"Unless the killer canvassed the area beforehand and knew the dead-times for traffic after midnight," Ellington offered.

"Any chance of video footage?" she asked.

"None. We checked. Agent Yardley even called some people—owners of the buildings closest by. But only one has security cameras and they are facing away from the church. So there's no dice there."

The other forensics member came over. He was carrying a medium-sized plastic bag that contained two large iron spikes and what looked like a thread of bailing wire. The spikes were coated in blood, which had also smeared itself along the clear interior of the bag.

"Are those railroad spikes?" Mackenzie asked.

"Probably," the forensics guy said. "But if they are, they're miniaturized ones. Maybe the kind people use to put up chicken coops or pasture fences."

"How long before you'll have any sort of results from these?" she asked.

The man shrugged. "Half a day, maybe? Let me know what you're looking for specifically and I'll try to get the results to you sooner."

"See if you can find out what the killer used to drive the spikes in. Can you tell that sort of thing by the recent wear on the spike heads?"

"Yeah, we should be able to do that. Everything has pretty much been handled on our end. The body is still with us; it won't get to the coroner until we say so. The doors and stoop have been dusted for prints. We'll let you know if we find anything."

"Thanks," Mackenzie said.

"Sorry to have already moved the body. But the sun was coming up and we really didn't want this in today's papers. Or tomorrow's for that matter."

"No, that's fine. I totally understand."

With that, Mackenzie turned back to the double doors, nonverbally dismissing the forensics team. She tried to picture someone lugging a body across the small lawn and up the stairs in the dead of night. The positioning of security lights on the street would make the front of the church dark. There were no lights of any kind along the front of the church, so it would have been cast in almost absolute darkness.

Maybe it would have been more possible than I originally thought for the killer to take all the time he needed to get this done, she thought.

"That seemed like a weird request," Ellington said. "What are you thinking?"

"I don't know yet. But I do know that it would take a hell of a lot of strength and determination to work by yourself in order to haul someone off of the ground just to nail their hands to these doors. If a sledgehammer was used to knock the nails in, it might denote more than one killer—one to hold the victim off the ground *and* extend the arm, and another to drive the nails in."

"Paints a hell of a picture, doesn't it?" Ellington said.

Mackenzie nodded as she started snapping pictures of the scene with her cell phone. As she did, the idea of crucifixion again crept up on her. It made her think of the first case she'd ever worked where themes of crucifixion had been utilized—a case back in Nebraska that had eventually led her to rub elbows with the bureau.

The Scarecrow Killer, she thought. *God, am I ever going to be able to leave that in the dust of my memory?*

Behind her, the sun started to rise, casting the first rays of light on the day. As her shadow was slowly cast upon the church steps, she tried to ignore the fact that it looked almost like a cross.

Again, memories of the Scarecrow Killer fogged her mind.

Maybe this will be it, she thought hopefully. *Maybe when I close this case, memories of those people crucified in the cornfields will stop haunting my memory.*

But as she looked back at those bloodstained doors of Cornerstone Presbyterian, she was afraid this was nothing more than wishful thinking.

CHAPTER THREE

Mackenzie learned a great deal about Reverend Ned Tuttle in the next half an hour. For starters, he had left behind two sons and a sister. His wife had walked out on him eight years ago, moving to Austin, Texas, with a man she had been having an affair with for over a year before it had come to light. Both sons lived in the Georgetown area, leading Mackenzie and Ellington to their first stop of the day. It was just after 6:30 when Mackenzie parked her car along the curb outside of Brian Tuttle's apartment. According to the agent who had broken the news, both brothers were there, waiting to do what they could to answer questions about their father's death.

When Mackenzie stepped into Brian Tuttle's apartment, she was a little surprised. She had expected to see two sons deep in grief, torn apart by the loss of their devout father. Instead, she saw them sitting at a small dining room table in the kitchen. They were both drinking coffee. Brian Tuttle, twenty-two years of age, was eating a bowl of cereal while Eddie Tuttle, nineteen, was absently dabbing an Eggo waffle into a pool of syrup.

"I don't exactly know what you're thinking we can offer you," Brian said. "We weren't exactly on the best terms with Dad."

"Can I ask why?" Mackenzie asked.

"Because we stopped associating with him when he went full-tilt into the church."

"Are you not believers?" Ellington asked.

"I don't know," Brian said. "I guess I'm an agnostic."

"I'm a believer," Eddie said. "But Dad...he took it to a whole different level. Like, when he found out Mom was cheating on him, he didn't do anything. After about two days of dealing with it, he forgave her *and* the guy she was cheating on him with. He said he forgave them because it was the Christian thing to do. And he refused to even talk about a divorce."

"Yeah," Brian said. "And Mom saw that as Dad not giving a shit about her—not caring that she had cheated. So she left. And he didn't do much of anything to stop her."

"Did your Dad ever try to reach out to the two of you since your mom left?"

"Oh yeah," Brian said. "Just about every Saturday evening, begging us to come to church."

"And besides that," Eddie added, "he was too busy during the week even if we *did* want to see him. He was always at the church or out on charity drives or sick visits at hospitals."

"When was the last time either of you spoke to him at length?" Mackenzie asked.

The brothers looked at each other for a moment, calculating. "Not sure," Brian said. "Maybe a month. And it wasn't much of anything. He was asking the same questions: how was work going, if I was dating anyone yet, stuff like that."

"So it's safe to say you both have an estranged relationship with your father?"

"Yeah," Eddie said.

He looked down to the table for a moment as regret started to sink in. Mackenzie had seen this sort of reaction before; if she'd been forced to bet, she was pretty sure at least one of these boys would be a sobbing mess within an hour, realizing all that had been lost in terms of the father they'd never gotten to know.

"Do you know who *would* have known him well?" Mackenzie asked. "Did he have any close friends?"

"Just that priest or pastor or whatever at the church," Eddie said. "The one that runs the place."

"Your father wasn't the lead reverend?" Mackenzie asked.

"No. He was like an associate pastor or something," Brian said. "There was another guy over him. Jerry Levins, I think."

Mackenzie noticed the way the young men were getting their terminology mixed up. Pastor, reverend, priest...it was all confusing. Mackenzie didn't even know the difference actually, assuming it had something to do with differences in beliefs between denominations.

"And your father spent a lot of time with him?"

"Oh yeah," Brian said, a bit angry. "All of his damn time, I think. If you need to know anything about Dad, he'd be the one to ask."

Mackenzie nodded, well aware that she would not be getting any useful information out of these two young men. Still, she wished she had more time to speak with them. There was clearly unresolved tension and loss between them. Maybe if they broke through whatever emotional walls were keeping them so tranquil, they'd have more to offer.

In the end, she turned away and gave them her thanks. She and Ellington left the apartment quietly. As they took the stairs down side by side, he took her hand.

"You okay?" he asked.

"Yeah," she said, confused. "Why?"

"Two kids…their father just died and aren't sure how to handle it. With all of the speculation about your dad's old case as of late…just wondering."

She smiled at him, reveling in the uplifting way he made her heart feel in those moments. *God, he can be so sweet…*

As they walked out into the morning together, she also realized that he was right: the reason she had wanted to stay and keep talking was to help the Tuttle brothers resolve the issues they'd had with their father.

Apparently, the ghost of her father's recently reopened case was haunting her more than she realized.

***

Seeing Cornerstone Presbyterian Church in the light of morning was surreal. Mackenzie drove by it on the way to visit with Reverend Jerry Levins. Levins resided in a house that sat just half a block away from the church, something Mackenzie had seen a lot of during her time out in Nebraska where the heads of smaller churches tended to live in very close proximity to their houses of worship.

When they arrived at Levins's house, there were numerous cars parked along the side of the street and in his driveway. She assumed these were likely members of Cornerstone, coming by to seek solace from or offer comfort to Reverend Levins.

When Mackenzie knocked on the front door of the modest little brick house, it was answered right away. The woman at the door had clearly been crying. She eyed Mackenzie and Ellington suspiciously until Mackenzie raised her badge.

"We're Agents White and Ellington, with the FBI," she said. "We'd like to speak with Reverend Levins, if he's in."

The woman opened the door for them and they stepped into a house that was filled with sniffling and sobbing. Somewhere else within the house, Mackenzie could hear the sound of murmured prayers.

"I'll get him for you," the woman said. "Please wait here."

Mackenzie watched the woman go back through the house, turning into a small living room where a few people stood by the

16

entryway. After some whispering noises, a tall bald man came walking toward them. Like the woman who had answered the door, he had also been weeping.

"Agents," Levins said. "Can I help you?"

"Well, I know it's a very tense and sad time for you," Mackenzie said, "but we're hoping to get any information we can on Reverend Tuttle. The sooner we can get any leads, the quicker we can catch who did this."

"Do you think his death is related to that poor priest's from earlier this week?" Levins asked.

"We can't know for certain yet," Mackenzie said, though she was already certain he was. "And that's why we were hoping you could speak with us."

"Of course," Levins said. "Outside on the stoop, though. I don't want to interrupt the prayer we have going here."

He led them back out into the morning, where he took a seat on the concrete steps. "I must say, I'm not sure what you're going to find on Ned," Levins commented. "He was a stand-up believer. Other than some issues with his family, I don't know that he had anything closely resembling an enemy."

"Did he have friends within the church that you might question being moral or upstanding?" Ellington asked.

"Everyone was friends with Ned Tuttle," Levins said, wiping a tear away from his eyes. "The man was as close to a saint as they come. He regularly tithed at least twenty-five percent of his pay back into the church. He was always downtown, helping to feed and clothe the poor. He mowed lawns for the elderly, did home repair for widows, took three missions trips to Kenya every year to help with a medical ministry."

"Do you know anything about his past that might be shady?" Mackenzie asked.

"No. And that's saying a lot because I know a great deal about his past. He and I, we shared a lot of stories about our struggles. And I can tell you in confidence that among the few sinful things he experienced in his past, there was nothing that would suggest being treated in the way he was last night."

"How about any people within the church?" Mackenzie asked. "Were there members of the church who might have been offended at something Reverend Tuttle said or did?"

Levins thought about it for only a moment before shaking his head. "No. If there was such an issue, Ned never told me and I never knew about it. But again…I can tell you with the utmost certainty that he had no enemies that I was aware of."

17

"Do you know if—" Ellington started.

But Levins held up his hand, as if shooing the comment away. "I'm very sorry," he said. "But I'm quite sad about the loss of my good friend, and I have many grieving members of my church inside. I will happily answer any questions you have in the coming days, but I need to report to God and my congregation right now."

"Of course," Mackenzie said. "I understand. And I am truly sorry for your loss."

Levins managed a smile as he got back to his feet. Fresh tears were streaming down his face. "I meant what I said," he whispered, doing what he could to not break down in front of them. "Give me a day or so. If there is anything further you need to ask, let me know. I'd like to take part in bringing whoever did this to justice."

With that, he headed back inside. Mackenzie and Ellington walked back to the car as the sun finally took its rightful place in the sky. It was hard to believe it was only 8:11.

"What next?" Mackenzie asked. "Any ideas?"

"Well...I've been awake for nearly four hours now and I haven't had coffee yet. That seems like a good place to start."

***

Twenty minutes later, Mackenzie and Ellington were sitting face to face in a small coffee shop. As they drank their coffee, they looked over the files on Father Costas they had taken from McGrath's office and the digital files on Reverend Tuttle that had been emailed to Mackenzie's phone.

Aside from studying the photographs, there was not really much to study. Even in the case of Father Costas, where there was paperwork to go along with it, there wasn't much to tell. He had been killed from either the puncture wound to his lung or a deep incision in the back of his neck that had gone deep enough to reveal white glimmers of his spine.

"So according to this report," Mackenzie said, "the wounds to Father Costas's body were likely what killed him. He was most likely dead before he was crucified."

"And that means something?" Ellington asked.

"I think there's a very good chance. It's clear there's some sort of religious angle here. The mere subject of crucifixion supports that. But there's a huge difference between using the *act* of crucifixion as a message and using the *imagery* of crucifixion."

"I think I follow," Ellington said. "But you can keep explaining."

18

"For Christians, the *image* of crucifixion would really just be a depiction of sorts. In our cases, death as a result of crucifixion doesn't seem to be the goal. If that were the case, the bodies would likely be mostly free of injury. Think about it...the whole of Christianity would be quite different if Christ was already dead when he was nailed to the cross."

"So you think the killer is crucifying these men just for show?"

"Too early to tell," Mackenzie said. She paused long enough to take a blissful gulp of her coffee. "I'm leaning toward *no,* though. Both men were men of the cloth...leaders of a church in some form or another. Displaying them strung up like the Christian figure those churches revolve around is too much of a sign. There's some sort of motive behind it all."

"You just referred to Jesus Christ as a Christian figure. I thought you believed in God."

"I do," Mackenzie said. "But not with the strength and conviction someone like Ned Tuttle had. And when it gets into the Bible stories—the talking snake, the ark, the blow-by-blow of the crucifixion—I think faith has to take a back seat and rely on something closer to blind belief. And I'm not comfortable with that."

"Whoa," Ellington said with a smile. "That's deep. Me...I just prefer to go with *I don't know* answer. So...as for the motive you mentioned. How do we find it?" Ellington asked.

"Good question. I plan to start with the family of Father Costas. There's not much to go on in the reports. Also, I think—"

She was interrupted by the ringing of Ellington's phone. He grabbed it quickly and frowned at what he saw on the display. "It's McGrath," he said before answering it.

Mackenzie listened to Ellington's end of the conversation, unable to piece together what was being said. After less than a minute, Ellington ended the call and shoved his phone back into his pocket.

"Well," he said. "It looks like you'll be visiting the Costas family on your own. McGrath needs me back at his office. Some detail work on a case he's being all secretive on."

"Which probably means it's grunt work," Mackenzie said. "Lucky you."

"Still...seems weird he'd yank me off of this so soon when we don't have any leads. It must mean he has immense confidence in you all of a sudden."

"And you don't?"

"You know what I mean," Ellington said, smiling.

Mackenzie took another gulp of her coffee, a little disgruntled to find that it was already empty. She tossed the cup in the trash and gathered up the files and her phone, ready to move in to her next stop. First, though, she headed for the counter to order another coffee.

It was looking like it was going to be a very long day. And without Ellington to keep her on her toes, she'd definitely need coffee.

Then again, long days usually resulted in leads—in productivity. And if Mackenzie had her way, she'd find the killer before he had time to so much as plan another murder.

CHAPTER FOUR

After dropping Ellington off in the parking garage at the FBI offices (and a quick yet passionate kiss before she left), Mackenzie made her way out to Blessed Heart Catholic Church. She wasn't expecting to find much of anything, so she wasn't disappointed when that was exactly what was waiting for her.

The doors had been replaced, but looked like exact replicas of the ones she had seen in the photos from the crime scene. She climbed up the stairs, these much fancier and ornate than the ones at Cornerstone Presbyterian, and to the new doors. She then turned her back to the doors and looked back out to the street. She couldn't help but wonder if there was any further symbolism in nailing the men to the front doors.

Maybe they're supposed to be looking out toward something, Mackenzie thought. But all she was seeing were parked cars, a few pedestrians, and street signs.

She looked at her feet and along the edges of the door frame. There were small spackled shapes there that could be anything. But she had seen this color before—the color of blood once it dried into pale concrete.

She looked back down the steps and tried to imagine a man bringing a dead body up them. It would be a task, that was for sure. Of course, she didn't know for sure that Costas had been dead when he had been nailed to the door, though that seemed to be the working assumption.

As she stood at the double doors and looked around, she went over the facts as she knew them from the files. *The same kind of nails were used here as were used at the Tuttle scene. The only common injury among the two bodies was a large gash that went the length of their foreheads—maybe an allusion to Christ's crown of thorns.*

Imagining such a grisly sight on the stoop she was standing on was hard to imagine. People didn't typically think of death and gore when they stood before the doors of a church.

And maybe that's the point. Maybe that's a tie-in to the killer's motive.

Feeling like she might be on to something, Mackenzie took the stairs back down to the street. It felt odd to be moving at such a pace without Ellington by her side, but by the time she was in her car and moving forward, her mind was solely on the case.

***

For the second time that day, Mackenzie found herself walking into a crowded home. Father Costas had lived in a nice home, a two-story brick home just along the outskirts of the downtown region. She was met by a woman who introduced herself as a parishioner of Blessed Heart. She led Mackenzie into a den area, where she was asked to wait for a moment.

Within a matter of seconds, an older woman entered the room. She looked exhausted and profoundly sad when she sat down in an armchair across from the seat Mackenzie had taken on an ornate sofa.

"I'm so sorry to bother you," Mackenzie said. "I had no idea you'd have this much company."

"Yes, I had no idea, either," the woman said. "But the funeral is tonight and there are all of these people coming out of the woodwork. Family members, acquaintances, loved ones from the church." She then grinned sleepily and added: "I'm Nancy Allensworth, the parish secretary. I'm told you're with the FBI?"

"Yes ma'am. At the risk of upsetting you further, there was another body discovered this morning, treated the same way as Father Costas. This one was a reverend at a small Presbyterian church near Georgetown."

Nancy Allensworth put her hand to her mouth in a dramatic *oh no* gesture. "My goodness," she said. Then, through tears and gritted teeth, she hissed, "What has this wretched world come to?"

Doing her best to press on, Mackenzie continued. "Obviously, we have reason to believe it could happen again if it has happened twice. So time is of the essence. I was hoping you might be able to answer a few questions for me."

"I can try," she said, though it was clear that she was struggling to keep her emotions in check.

"Because Blessed Heart is a relatively large church, I was wondering if there might have been someone within the congregation who might have recently approached Father Costas with a complaint or grievance."

"Not that I'm aware of. Of course, keep in mind that many people came to him in confidence to confess sins or work out spiritual unrest within their lives."

"Is there anything at all over the course of the last several years that you can think of that might have rubbed someone the wrong way? Anything that might upset someone who perhaps previously looked at Father Costas with reverence?"

Nancy looked down at her hands. She was wringing them nervously in her lap, trying to keep them from trembling. "I suppose there was, but it was before I started working here. There was a story maybe ten years back, a report that one of the local papers broke. One of the teenage boys that lead a youth group claimed that Father Costas had sexually abused him. It was very explicit. There was never any proof of it and, quite frankly, there's just no way Father Costas would have done that. But once a news story like that hits and concerns someone within the Catholic Church, it's taken as solid truth."

"What was the aftermath of that story?"

"From what I was told, he got death threats. Attendance at the church decreased by about fifteen percent. He started to receive unsolicited emails filled with homosexual pornography."

"Did he keep any of those mails?" Mackenzie asked.

"For a while," Nancy said. "He had the cops called in on it but they were never able to make any connections. After it was clear that nothing was going to be able to be done, he deleted them all. I've never seen them personally."

"And what about the teen who made the accusations? If you could give us his name, we could pay him a visit."

Nancy shook her head, fresh tears spilling. "He committed suicide later that year. There was a note near the body where he confessed to being gay. It was yet another strike against Father Costas. It made the story seem all that more plausible."

Mackenzie nodded, trying to think of any other accessible avenues. She knew, naturally, that trying to get this sort of information out of a grieving widow would be difficult. And when you added in a past ordeal with a news story that may or may not have had any truth to it, the whole thing just became that much worse. She supposed she could push for more information about the young man who had filed the complaint and eventually killed himself. But she could also easily find that information on her own while leaving this poor woman to get ready for Father Costas's funeral.

"Well, Ms. Allensworth, thank you so much for your time," Mackenzie said, getting to her feet. "My deepest sympathies for your loss."

"Bless you, my dear," Nancy said. She also got to her feet and led Mackenzie back through the house, to the front door.

At the door, Mackenzie gave Nancy a business card with her name and number on it. "I understand you are going through quite a lot," Mackenzie said. "But if anything else should happen to come to you in the next few days, please give me a call."

Nancy took the card without a word and slipped it into her pocket. She then turned away, clearly fighting back a larger swarm of tears, and closed the door.

Mackenzie headed back to her car, pulling out her cell phone. She dialed up Agent Harrison, who answered right away.

"Everything going well?" he asked her.

"I don't know yet," she said. "Can you do me a favor and look back about ten years to see what you can find about Father Costas being accused of sexually abusing a male leader of a youth group? I'd like as many details on the case as I can get."

"Sure. You think it might present a lead?"

"I don't know," she said. "But I think a kid who claims to have been sexually abused by a priest who was nailed to the door of his church would certainly be worth looking into."

"Yeah, good point," Harrison said.

She ended the call, again haunted by images of the Scarecrow Killer and Nebraska. She had obviously dealt with killers striking out of a religious context before. And one thing she knew about them was that they could be unpredictable and very driven. She wasn't going to take any chances and, as such, would not leave any stone unturned.

Yet as she got back into her car, she realized that a sexually abused boy *did* feel like a solid lead. Besides, other than him, the only thing at her disposal was returning to the FBI offices and seeing what she could mine from the files while hoping Forensics might be able to come up with something.

And she knew that if she sat idly, waiting for a break in the case, the killer could very well be out there plotting his next move.

CHAPTER FIVE

It was 3:08 by the car's dashboard when the pastor came out of the church.

He watched the pastor through the windshield from a distance. He knew the man was holy; his reputation was stellar and his church had been blessed. Still, it was rather disappointing. Sometimes he thought holy men should be set apart from the rest of the world, easier to identify. Maybe like those old religious paintings where Jesus had a large golden circle around his head.

He chuckled at the thought of this as he watched the pastor meet with another man in front of a car by the church. This other man was an assistant of some sort. He'd seen this assistant before but wasn't concerned with him. He was very low on the food chain within the church.

No, he was more interested in the head pastor.

He closed his eyes as the two men talked. In the silence of his car, he prayed. He knew he could pray anywhere and God would hear him. He had known for quite some time that God did not care where you were when you prayed or confessed your sins. You did not have to be in some huge and gaudily decorated building. In fact, the Bible indicated that such elaborate dwellings were an affront to God.

With his prayer over, he thought about that bit of scripture. He muttered it out loud, his voice slow and gritty.

"And when thou prayest, thou shalt not be as the hypocrites are. For they love to pray standing in the synagogues and in the corners of the streets, so that they may be seen of men."

He looked back to the pastor, currently walking away from the man and to another car.

"Hypocrite," he said. His voice was a mixture of venom and sadness.

He also knew that the Bible warned of a plague of false prophets in the end times. That was, after all, why he had set himself to his current task. The false prophets, the men who spoke of glorifying God while eyeing the collection plates as they were passed around—the same ones who preached of sanctification and purity while staring at young boys with lustful eyes—they were the

25

worst of them. They were worse than the drug dealers and murderers. They were worse than rapists and the most deplorable deviants on the streets.

Everyone knew it. But no one did anything about it.

Until now. Until he had heard God speaking into him, telling him to set it right.

It was his job to rid the world of these false prophets. It was bloody work, but it was God's work. And that was all he needed to know.

He looked back to the pastor, getting into his car and leaving the church.

After a while, he also pulled out onto the street. He did not tail the pastor closely, but followed along at a safe distance.

When he came to a stoplight, he could just barely hear the musical noise from his trunk as several of his industrial nails clinked together in their box.

CHAPTER SIX

She walks up toward the church, the blood moon casting a shadow of her body on the sidewalk that looks like a stretched out bug—a praying mantis or a millipede perhaps. There is a bell ringing, a large bell above the cathedral, summoning everyone to come worship and sing and give praise.

But Mackenzie cannot get inside the church. There is a throng of people on the front stoop, congregating around the front door. She sees Ellington there, as well as McGrath, Harrison, her estranged mother and sister, even her old partner, Bryers, and some of the men she'd worked with while still a detective back in Nebraska.

"What's everyone doing?" she asks.

Ellington turns to her. His eyes are closed. He is dressed in a nice suit, punctuated by a blood red tie. He smiles at her, his eyes still closed, and holds a hand to his lips. Beside him, her mother points to the front doors of the church.

Her father is there. Strung up, crucified. He wears a crown of thorns, and a wound in his side leaks something that looks like motor oil. He is looking directly at her, his eyes wide and maniacal. He is insane. She can see it in his eyes and in the leer of a grin.

"Has thee come to save thyself?" he asks her.

"No," she says.

"Well, you certainly did not come to save me. Too late for that. Now bow. Worship. Find your peace in me."

And as if someone has broken her in half from inside, Mackenzie kneels. She kneels hard, scraping her knees on the concrete. All around her, the congregation starts to sing in tongues. She opens her mouth and formless words come out, joining in the song. She looks back up to her father and there is a halo of fire encircling his head. He is dead now, his eyes blank and expressionless, his mouth trailing a pool of blood.

There is the chiming of the bell, repeating over and over again.

Ringing...

Ringing. Something ringing.

Her phone. With a jerk, Mackenzie came awake. She barely registered the clock on her bedside table, which read 2:10 a.m. She

27

answered the phone, trying to shake the vestiges of the nightmare from her head

"This is White," she said.

"Good morning," came Harrison's voice. She was secretly rather disappointed. She'd been expecting to hear from Ellington. He'd been sent off on some task by McGrath, the details of which were sketchy at best. He'd promised to call at some point but so far, she'd heard nothing from him.

Harrison, she thought groggily. *What the hell does he want?*

"It's way too early for this, Harrison," she said.

"I know," Harrison said. "Sorry, but I'm calling for McGrath. There's been another murder."

***

Through a series of texts, Mackenzie pieced together all she needed to know. A rebellious couple had pulled off into the shadow of a well-known church's parking lot to have sex. Just as things had started heating up, the girl had seen something strange on the door. It had spooked her enough to put an end to the night's planned activities. Clearly pissed, the male who had been robbed of his exhibitionism stalked to the front door and found a naked body nailed to the doors.

The church in question was a fairly popular one: Living Word Community Church, one of the largest in the city. It often made the news, as the President frequently attended services there. Mackenzie had never been (she had not stepped into a church since a guilt-filled weekend in college) but the size and scope of the place sank in fully as she steered her car into the parking lot.

She was one of the first on the scene. The CSI team was there, approaching the main entrance of the church. A single agent was getting out of a car, apparently having been waiting for her. She was not at all surprised to see that it was Yardley, the agent who had handled the first case with Father Costas.

Yardley met her at the sidewalk that led to the main entrance. She looked tired but excited in a way that only other agents would likely identify and relate to.

"Agent White," Yardley said. "Thanks for coming so quickly."

"Sure. Were you the first one on the scene?"

"I was. I got sent out about fifteen minutes ago. Harrison called and sent me."

Mackenzie almost commented on this but shut it down. *Strange that I wasn't called first,* she thought. *Maybe McGrath is letting her fill in where Ellington would be helping. Makes sense, as she was the first to handle the Costas scene.*

"Seen the body yet?" Mackenzie asked as they headed for the front door just behind the CSI team.

"Yeah. From a few feet away. It's identical to the others."

Within a few steps, Mackenzie was able to see this for herself. She stayed back a bit, letting the CSI and Forensics guys do their job. Sensing that they had two agents behind them waiting, the teams worked quickly yet efficiently, making sure to leave the two agents some room to take in their own observations.

Yardley was right. The scene *was* the same, right down to the elongated mark across the brow. The only difference was that this man's underwear had apparently slipped down—or had been yanked down to his ankles on purpose.

One of the guys from the CSI team looked back at them. He looked a little out of sorts, maybe even a little sad.

"The deceased is Robert Woodall. He's the head pastor here."

"You're sure?" Mackenzie asked.

"Positive. My family attends this church. I've heard this man preach at least fifty times."

Mackenzie stepped closer to the body. The doors to Living Word were not ornate and decorative like the ones at Cornerstone Presbyterian and Blessed Heart. These were more modern, made of a heavy-duty wood that was designed and distressed to look like something akin to a barn door.

Like the others, Pastor Woodall had been nailed through the hands and his ankles had been bound with bailing wire. She studied his exposed genitalia, wondering if his stark nakedness had been a decision made by the killer who had staged the body. She could see nothing out of the ordinary and decided that the underwear must have slid down by itself, perhaps due to the weight of the blood it had collected. The wounds that had shed that blood were numerous. There were a few scratches on his chest. And while his back could not be seen, the trails of blood that smeared along his waist and ventured down his legs indicated that there would be a few back there.

Mackenzie then saw another wound—a thin one that brought back the hellish imagery of her nightmare.

There was a slit in Woodall's right side. It was slight but clearly visible. There was something precise about it, almost pristine. She leaned in closer and pointed. "What's this look like to you?" she asked the CSI team.

"I noticed that, too," said the man who had recognized Pastor Woodall. "Looks like some sort of incision. Maybe made by some sort of crafting blade—an X-Acto knife or something."

"But these other cuts and stab wounds," Mackenzie said. "They're made with a standard blade, right? The angles and edges…"

"Yeah. You a religious woman?" the man asked.

"That seems to be a recurring question over the last day or so," she said. "Despite the answer, though, I understand the relevance of a cut to the side. It's where Christ was speared while he was hanging on the cross."

"Yeah," Yardley said from behind her. "But there was no blood, right?"

"Right," Mackenzie said. "According to scripture, water came out of this wound."

So why did the killer decide to make this wound stand out? she wondered. *And why was it not on the others?*

She stood back and observed the scene while Yardley chatted with a few of the CSI and Forensics members. The case had already unnerved her a bit but this random wound in Woodall's side made her worry that something deeper might be going on. There was symbolism but then there was *layered* symbolism.

The killer has obviously thought things out, she thought. *He has a plan and he's being methodical about it. More than that, the addition of this very precise cut in the side shows that he's not just killing to kill — he's trying to convey a message.*

"But what message?" she asked herself quietly.

In the darkest hours of night, she stood in the entryway to Living Word Community Church and tried to find that message on the canvas of the dead pastor's body.

CHAPTER SEVEN

In the time it had taken Mackenzie to leave Living Word and drive to the J. Edgar Hoover building, the media had somehow found out about the newest murder. While the murder of Father Costas had made the news, the death of Ned Tuttle had not. But with the lead pastor of a church with the status of Living Word, the case was going to blow up the headlines. It was 4:10 when Mackenzie arrived at the FBI offices, headed up to see McGrath. She figured that the details of Pastor Woodall and the case as a whole would be the main point of interest on local morning news programs—and all over the nation by noon.

She could feel the mounting pressure of it all as she stepped into McGrath's office. He was sitting at his little conference table, on the phone with someone. Agent Harrison was there with him, reading something from a laptop. Yardley was also there, having arrived a scant few minutes before Mackenzie. She was sitting, listening to McGrath on the phone, apparently awaiting instruction.

Seeing the two of them hovering around McGrath made her wish Ellington was here. It reminded her that she was still in the dark about where McGrath had sent him. She wondered if it had something to do with this case—but if it did, why had she not been informed of his whereabouts?

When McGrath finally got off the phone, he looked to the three gathered agents and let out a sigh. "That was Assistant Director Kirsch," he said. "He's assembling three more agents to spearhead this case on his end. The moment the media caught wind of this, we were fucked. This is going to go big and it's going to go big quickly."

"Any particular reason?" Harrison asked.

"Living Word is a hugely popular church. The President goes there. A few other politicians are regulars, too. Their podcast gets around five hundred thousand listens a week. Woodall wasn't like a celebrity or anything, but he was well known. And if it's a church the President attends…"

"Got it," Harrison said.

McGrath looked at Mackenzie and Yardley. "Anything of note at the scene?"

"Yeah, maybe," Mackenzie said. She then went into detail about the peculiar and precise incision in Woodall's right side. She did not, however, go into what sort of symbolic gesture she was trying to decipher from its meaning. She had no real solid theories just yet and did not want to waste time with speculation.

McGrath, however, was in panic mode. He spread his hands out on the table and nodded to the chairs around the table. "Take a seat. Let's go over what we have. I want to be able to give Kirsch the same information we have. Including you three, we now have six agents dedicated to this case. If we work together, armed with the same details, we might be able to nab this guy before he strikes again."

"Well," Yardley said, "he's not sticking to one denomination. We know that for sure. If anything, it seems like he's trying to *avoid* that. So far we've got a Catholic church, a Presbyterian church, and now a nondenominational community church."

"And another thing to consider," Mackenzie said, "is that we can't know for certain if he's using the position of crucifixion as his preferred use of punishment and symbolism, or if he's doing it as a mockery."

"What's the difference, really?" Harrison asked.

"Until we know which reason is behind it, we can't narrow down the motive," Mackenzie said. "If he's doing it as a mockery, then he's likely not a believer—maybe even some sort of very angry atheist or former believer. But if he's doing it as a preferred means of symbolism, then he could be a very devout believer, albeit with some pretty strange ways to profess his faith."

"And this thin cut along Woodall's side," McGrath said. "It wasn't on any of the other bodies?"

"No," Mackenzie said. "It was new. Which makes me think it has some meaning to it. Like the killer might even be trying to communicate something to us. Or just going further off the rails."

McGrath pushed himself away from the table and looked to the ceiling, as if searching for answers up there. "I'm not blind to all of this," he said. "I know there are zero clues and no real avenues to pursue. But if I don't have *something* resembling a lead by the time this shit is splashed all over national news programs within a few hours, things are going to get bad around here. Kirsch says he's already gotten a call from a congresswoman who attends Living Word asking why we weren't able to crack this one as soon as Costas was killed. So I need the three of you to get me something. If I have nothing new to go on by this afternoon, I have to open it open wider…more resources, more manpower, And I really don't want to do that."

"I can check in with Forensics," Yardley offered.

"Work alongside them for all I care,' McGrath said. "I'll make a call and okay it. I want you there the moment they discover anything from those bodies."

"It might be a needle-in-a-haystack scenario," Harrison said, "but I can start looking at local hardware stores to get records and receipts about anyone who has purchased the nails this guy is using in the last few months. From what I understand, they aren't particularly common."

McGrath nodded. It was an idea, sure, but the look on his face made it clear how much time that would take.

"And you, White?" he asked.

"I'll go the families and co-workers," she said. "In a church the size of Living Word, there's got to be *someone* with some insight as to why this happened to Woodall."

McGrath clapped his hands together loudly and sat forward. "Sounds good," he said. "So get to it. And check in with me every hour on the hour. Got it?"

Yardley and Harrison nodded. Harrison closed his laptop as he stood up from the table. As they made their exit, Mackenzie hung back. When Yardley had closed the door behind them, leaving only Mackenzie and McGrath in the room, she turned back to him.

"Ah hell, what is it?" McGrath asked.

"I'm curious," she said. "Agent Ellington would have been a valuable asset for this case. Where did you send him off to?"

McGrath shifted uncomfortably in his seat and briefly looked out the window of his office, to the early morning darkness outside.

"Well, before I tasked him with this other assignment, I obviously had no idea this case was going to be this bad. As for where he is currently working, with all due respect, that's none of your business."

"With the same respect," she replied, doing her best not to sound too defensive, "you took away a partner I work well with, which leaves me on my own to work this case out."

"You are not on your own," McGrath said. "Harrison and Yardley are more than efficient. Now…please, Agent White. Get to work."

She wanted to press the issue further but didn't see the point. The last thing she needed was for McGrath to be pissed at her. The pressure was already on and it was *far* too early in the day to be dealing with a disgruntled boss.

33

She gave a curt little nod and took her leave. Still, as she walked toward the elevators, she pulled out her phone. It was too early to call Ellington so she opted for a text.

Just checking in, she typed. **Call or text when you can.**

She sent the text as she stepped into the elevator. She rode down to the garage where her car was waiting. Outside, the morning was still dark—the kind of thick darkness that seemed capable of hiding any secrets it wanted.

CHAPTER EIGHT

After grabbing a cup of coffee, Mackenzie headed back out to Living Word. She knew that it was a large church, so singling out anyone with possible information from within its staff or congregation would take forever. She figured that if the news had gotten out and phone calls had started to make the rounds, there was a very good chance that those close to Pastor Woodall would be at the church—perhaps already setting up little memorials or just coming to the church to be closer to God as they grieved.

Her intuition paid off yet again. When she arrived at the scene, Woodall had been removed from the doors. And while there were still several local police and members of the bureau present, there were also other people scattered here and there, held back by yellow crime scene tape that bordered the edge of the concrete walkway that led to the front doors.

A few of them were openly crying. Several were wrapped in the embraces of other onlookers. She took note of one man standing by himself, his head turned away from the scene. His head was lowered and his mouth was moving just slightly as he offered up prayers. Mackenzie respectfully gave him some time to finish his prayer before she approached him. As she neared him, she saw what looked to be an expression of anger on his face.

Excuse me, sir," she said. "Do you have a moment?" She finished her question by showing her ID and introducing herself.

"Yes," the man said. He blinked and rubbed at his eyes, as if trying to swipe away the last remnants of sleep or a bad dream. He then offered his hand and said, "I'm Dave Wylerman, by the way. I'm head of the music department here at Living Word."

"There's a music department?"

"Yeah. We have a rotating ensemble of about fourteen musicians that make up three worship bands."

"So you've worked closely with Pastor Woodall in the past?"

"Oh, absolutely. I'm in meetings with him at least twice a week. Outside of that, he's become a dear family friend to my wife, my kids, and I over the past decade or so."

"Can you think of anyone who might have been capable of doing this? Anyone who might have some sort of a grudge or grievance against Pastor Woodall?"

"Well, it's a big church. I don't think there's a single person that works here that knows *everyone* that attends. But as for me, no, I can't think of anyone right off the top of my head who was angry enough with him to do *this*..."

The early morning darkness had hidden Dave Wylerman's tears to this point, but when he looked up into her eyes they were quite clear. He looked troubled, as if he were struggling to figure out how to say something.

"Do you have a moment to talk in private?" Mackenzie asked.

"Yeah."

She waved him forward to follow her. She stepped away from the concrete entryway to the church and headed back to her car. She opened the passenger's side door for him, figuring it might do him some good to get off his feet and feel relaxed. She got in the driver's side and when she closed her door, she could tell that Wylerman was struggling to keep himself together.

"Has the rest of the church body been informed?" Mackenzie asked.

"No, just the elders, myself, and a few of those close to Pastor Woodall. But calls are being made. Everyone will know within an hour or so, I'd imagine."

Good, Mackenzie thought. *They'll personally receive the news from someone they know rather than hearing about it for the first time on the news.*

"So, correct me if I'm wrong," she said, "but it looked like you were struggling with something back there by the church. Is there something you can tell me that you didn't want to share in front of everyone else?"

"Well, as you know, it's a big church. On any given Sunday, if you count both services we hold, there's anywhere between five thousand and seven thousand people that attend. And with such a large group, we require several elders to handle the business and concerns of the church. Here at Living Word, we have six—well, we *had* six. One of them had started to sort of raise some concerns among the others before he left. I don't think he would have it in him to do something like this but...I don't know. Some things he had been insinuating...it sort of caught everyone else off guard. Other elders...employees..."

"What's his name?"

"Eric Crouse."

"And what sort of things?" Mackenzie asked.

"He kept spouting off about how things left in the dark will come to the light and how that light could be blinding. That maybe being burned by the light is exactly what Living Word needed."

"And how long had he been behaving this way?"

"About a month or so, I'd say. From what I understand, he left of his own accord about two weeks ago but there was talk before that among the other elders and Pastor Woodall about releasing him. But the thing of it is that everything Eric was saying was scripturally accurate. Things Jesus said, things that most people that attend Living Word believe. But…and I know this is going to sound dumb…it was the *way* he said the things. You know? Like, he had some hidden context to them. More than that, he never spoke like that before. He was an elder, sure, but never one to just spout off scripture or starting giving these hellfire-and-brimstone-type talks."

"So if you don't think he was capable of murder, why are you mentioning him? Was it just the sudden personality change that alarmed everyone?"

Wylerman shrugged. "No. Some people started to notice that Eric was doing everything he could to avoid meetings or small groups where Pastor Woodall would be in attendance. They've never been best friends, but always got along. Then all of a sudden, when he started talking about all of this light shining in the darkness stuff, he also seemed to distance himself from Pastor Woodall."

"And you say he left the church two weeks ago?"

"Yeah, give or take a few days. I don't know if he's attending somewhere else now or what. And what's strange is that it's almost as if Eric knew Pastor Woodall's schedule. He had just gotten back from a retreat a few days ago."

"A retreat?"

"Yeah, it's this little getaway he takes twice a year. It's a really quiet little island off the coast of Florida."

"And how long had he been back?" Mackenzie asked.

"He and his wife got back home five days ago."

Mackenzie thought about this for a moment, cataloguing it in her mind. She then turned matters back to the man Wylerman had mentioned—the former elder, Eric Crouse.

"Would you happen to know where Crouse lives?" she asked.

"Yeah. I've been in his house a few times for small groups and prayer."

Mackenzie wasn't sure why, but something about this creeped her out. The timing of Eric Crouse leaving Living Word was nearly perfect for the type of suspect she was looking for. To imagine this grieving man clasping praying hands together with a man who might have been responsible for three deaths over the last few days was unsettling.

"Can you tell me where?"

"I will," Wylerman said, "but I'd really rather you not tell him that you got the information from me...or anyone else at Living Word, for that matter."

"Of course not," she said.

A bit reluctantly, Wylerman gave her directions to Eric Crouse's house. Mackenzie typed them in on her phone, noticing that while Wylerman might have been interacting with her, his mind was very much still with his grieving friends out by the church. He was looking in that direction now, wiping tears from his eyes as he looked at them through the passenger window.

"Thanks for your time, Mr. Wylerman," Mackenzie said.

Wylerman nodded without saying anything else. He then got out of the car. He hung his head low before he even reached the small crowd of people. She could see him trembling. She had never understood how people could have deep faith in an invisible God, but she did respect the sense of community that was evident among those who shared a common belief. She felt very bad for Dave Wylerman in that moment, as well as those who attended Living Word and the void they would feel on Sunday morning.

With that sense of sympathy pushing her, Mackenzie pulled out of the Living Word lot and headed west, to what looked to be the first solid lead this case had churned up.

CHAPTER NINE

It was 6:40 when she arrived in front of Eric Crouse's home. It was located in a well-to-do neighborhood where the houses were more important than yards, each house pressed in tightly against the other. The garage was closed, making it impossible to know if anyone was home—though given the early hour, she assumed there would be someone there to answer the door.

As she made her way to his door, Mackenzie wished she'd picked up another coffee from somewhere. It was hard to believe that it was not yet seven o'clock. She did her best to shake the vestiges of sleep from her face as she rang the doorbell of the Crouse residence. Right away she could hear footfalls behind the door. Seconds later, the door opened just a crack and a woman peered out.

"Can I help you?" the woman asked, clearly suspicious.

"Yes," Mackenzie said. "And I do apologize for the early hour, but this is pressing. I'm Agent Mackenzie White with the FBI. I'm looking for Eric Crouse."

The woman slowly opened the door. "That's my husband. He's…well, he's received some terrible news this morning. I assume that's why you're here? About the murder this morning?"

"It is," she said. "So if I could speak with him…"

"Of course," the woman said. "Come in, come in."

Mackenzie was ushered inside to the smell of cooking bacon and freshly brewed coffee. The Crouse home was beautiful not overly so. There were high ceilings, crown molding, hardwood floors, and granite counters and a bar space in the kitchen. In the kitchen, the woman led her to a large dining room table; this was the type of kitchen that served as a dining room as well. A man and a boy of about ten sat at the table. The boy was eating a bowl of cereal while the man sipped at a cup of coffee and read something from a laptop.

"This lady is here from the FBI," Crouse's wife said.

Crouse looked up, blinking in a *what's going on* kind of way. He then got up and walked to Mackenzie. He smiled tiredly at her and she could see from his face that he, just like Dave Wylerman, had been doing his fair share of crying this morning.

39

Crouse extended his hand for a shake and Mackenzie obliged. She watched his face the entire time, looking for some flaw in what was either a great disguise of emotion or a front to fool her. She could not see either and, therefore, could not decide if he was hiding any guilt.

"I assume this is about Pastor Woodall?" Eric asked.

"Yes," Mackenzie said. "Is there somewhere we could talk?"

"Um, yeah," Eric said. He looked at his son and patted him on the shoulder. "Can you and Mommy run to the bathroom and finish getting ready for school? Get those teeth good, okay?"

The boy looked at his cereal, clearly not finished, but obeyed his father. So did the wife, as she escorted their son out of the kitchen and toward a hallway that sat off to the right. When they were out of sight, Eric looked at the coffee pot on the counter and asked: "Coffee?"

"Yes, please. That would be fantastic, actually."

Eric walked into the kitchen and Mackenzie followed. Eric grabbed a cup from a cupboard and filled it with coffee from the pot on the counter. "Cream? Sugar?"

"Black is fine," she said. She was pretty sure he was stalling, but at the same time, also trying his best to seem pleasant and hospitable.

When he handed her the coffee, she gave her thanks and sipped. It was good and strong—just what she needed.

"So, how did you find out about Pastor Woodall?" she asked.

"I got a call from one of the elders. I suppose if you're here to speak with me, you already know that I was an elder there until very recently."

"Yes. I was aware. And I understand there was a bit of hostility and disagreement just before you left."

"Yes, I suppose so."

"Would you care to elaborate on what you meant by the comments you made about the dark and the light? About Living Word being burned by the light?"

Eric hesitated, taking a drink from his coffee. "You see, the difficult thing here is that had you asked me that very same question yesterday, I would have gladly answered you. But things are different now."

"Well, Mr. Crouse, I had no reason to ask you that yesterday. But right now, I have a dead pastor that you were disagreeing with rather harshly…a pastor you worked closely with for several years and suddenly started to apparently not care for very much."

"That's fair," he said. He leaned to the right a bit, peering down the hallway as if to make sure his wife and son were still out of earshot. When he was confident that they were still gone, he stepped closer to Mackenzie. "Look…I discovered something about Pastor Woodall three months ago. At first, I refused to believe it but then I saw proof. And I couldn't deny it anymore. I…well, I guess I didn't know quite how to handle it."

"And what did you discover?"

"Agent White…he's dead. *Recently* dead. What kind of man would I be to speak ill of him? The last thing I want is to smear his name after he's dead."

"I'll keep it discreet then," she said. "No one other than my supervisor and two or three additional agents will know."

"I have your word on that?"

"Yes," she said. "Although, from what I understand, you wouldn't have cared much about dragging his name through the mud a few weeks ago."

Eric actually sneered at this. "You expect this shit from small-town churches…rumors and gossip. Yes…I probably did not do the best job at staying quiet. I said some not-so-subtle things that might have raised eyebrows. But believe me…with what I know, I could have gone public. I could have smeared his name right away. But I didn't."

"And why not?"

"Because it's not my job to judge. He's dead now and God will judge him."

"Judge him for what?" Mackenzie asked. "What's the big secret?"

His eyes were welling with tears as he spoke and it was that one simple indicator that told Mackenzie that Eric Crouse was not only not the killer, but that despite his recent behavior, he *had* once cared for Pastor Woodall.

"I had a young man come to me in confidence about three months ago. From time to time, I'd help with the teen classes at Living Word. This was a kid I'd talked to off and on when he was younger…sort of helped him with his spiritual journey, answered the tough God questions, things like that. So he comes to me and it's been…I don't know…maybe a year since I've had a real conversation with him. He asks if we can talk in private, so I took him to my office. He tells me that for the last year or so, he's been having a homosexual relationship. So I'm prepared to talk it out with him, to see where he's at mentally and everything. But then he finishes the comment…the relationship was with Pastor Woodall."

41

"And you believed him, just like that?" Mackenzie asked.

"Hell no. It actually made me mad that the guy would even insinuate such a thing. But then he showed me his cell phone. There were texts and pictures. And I hated him for showing it to me. I hated *him* for it and not Woodall."

"Did you tell anyone?"

"No. I didn't know what the hell to do. If I exposed him, that could be the end of Living Word. And besides that, the guy asked me *not* to. He'd just wanted to come to me about it to confess his sins. But in the back of my head and heart, I always thought he'd told me about it with a quiet hope that I *would* go public. Some of those messages were...well, they insinuated abuse."

"How so?"

"The guy was wanting out of it. And Woodall told him if he stopped seeing him or told anybody about what was happening, he'd start spreading lies about the guy. There were some other things that were said that sort of suggested unwanted sex. Maybe not rape, but...ah God. This is terrible."

"You're sure about all of this?"

Eric nodded. The tears were flowing now, dropping from his face. "I'm glad you came. God, I needed to tell someone and—"

He bit back a sob here and looked down at the floor.

"Mr. Crouse...please understand that I *have* to speak to this young man."

"I can't give you his name. I can't..."

"Mr. Crouse...Pastor Woodall is one of three religious leaders that have been brutally killed within eight days. This is a serial case and we have no way of knowing who is next. Any and every lead I have at my disposal, I need to use. And speaking to a boy who could very well be a victim of abuse at the hands of the most recently murdered religious figure is too in-your-face to ignore. At the risk of just tossing guilt at you, your refusal to provide a name could very well hinder this investigation and lead to more deaths."

"Chris Marsh," Eric said, the name coming from his mouth like a strangled hiss of pain. And then he let out a moan of anguish that was nearly as loud as a scream.

This was followed by the sound of his wife from the back of the house. She was running through the hallway, calling his name. When she reached the kitchen, she gave Mackenzie a look of pure venom.

"What happened?" she asked, nearly screaming at Mackenzie.

"Not her fault," Eric managed to say. "But oh God, there's...there's something I have to tell you..."

There was no graceful way to make an exit. Mackenzie gave a thanks that was drowned out by Eric Crouse's grief. When she left the house she did so without any fanfare. The wife gave her only the most half-hearted of waves as she headed for the front door.

As she closed it behind her, all she saw was their ten-year-old son, creeping back down the hallway to see why his father was crying so loud.

In every case, Mackenzie felt there was one thing she would see or hear from someone that lit a fuse in her—that made her more determined than ever to bring a case to a close.

For this case, it was the sight of that uncertain little boy walking down the hall, hearing his father cry from the result of horrors he did not yet know and probably would not understand. The boy wasn't even aware that Mackenzie had spotted him but she burned that image into her mind as she bounded down the Crouses' porch steps and back to her car.

As she reached the car, her phone rang from within her coat pocket. She took it out and her heart managed the slightest bit of joy when she saw the name **Ellington** on the display.

She answered the call, doing her best not to sound as relieved as she actually was. "Ah, so you *didn't* forget about me!"

"Of course I didn't."

"All jokes aside," Mackenzie said, "McGrath got you out of town pretty quickly. And he wouldn't tell me a damned thing. What's he got you working on anyway?"

She was in her car now, starting the engine. Even over that sound, though, she was able to clearly hear Ellington's deep sigh. "Yeah, I figured he'd leave that part to me."

"What's that mean? Ellington, what's going on?"

"Early yesterday morning, the Omaha, Nebraska, field office called McGrath. One of the agents down there is working with a private investigator, sort of under the radar and—"

"Is it Kirk Peterson?" she interrupted.

"Yeah. There's been some movement on that newer case that's linked to your father."

"What the hell, Ellington?"

"I know. But look…I think he was right to tell me and not you. I'm pretty much done here. It was a weak-ass lead and came to basically nothing. It made more sense for me to come. I'm not personally attached to it and, let's face it, you're the smarter choice to stay there and work on this current case. It sucks and I'm sorry he chose to keep you in the dark on it. But you're going to realize in about an hour or so that this was the smartest play."

"Well, maybe we should save this conversation for an hour from now," she spat. The hell of it was that he was right. It *was* the smarter move.

"Or we can wait until I get back. I should be wrapped up by tonight. Maybe sooner. I don't see why I won't be back in DC by tomorrow afternoon sometime."

"This sucks," she said, hating the simplistic and childish way it sounded.

"It does," he said. "But I promise…you missed nothing. I'll let you read the case files when I get back. I'll even let you see them before I hand them in to McGrath."

"Yeah, I don't think he'll like that."

"Well, he made me keep a secret from you yesterday. So I guess you and I will just hide one from him."

She did feel betrayed at the situation but also knew that to voice it and get into an argument over the phone would do absolutely nothing. If anything, it would only set her back in regards to the current case. And she would not allow herself to be tripped up in such a way.

"Okay. But yes…I want to read those case files when you get back."

"Cross my heart. It's looking like I should be back sometime late tonight. I'll let you know when I get back."

When they ended the call, it took everything within Mackenzie not to call up McGrath right away and ask him just what in the hell he thought he was doing. Ellington was right; sending her to Nebraska would have certainly slowed down her current case…but she still felt slighted —like she had been left in the dark on purpose.

Shoving that down, she pulled out into the street. She pushed away all feelings of anger and betrayal, replacing them with the image of the Crouse's son, slowly creeping back down the hall toward the sound of his wailing father.

CHAPTER TEN

After making a quick information request over the phone to the bureau, Mackenzie got an address for Chris Marsh. It just happened to be the same address for his parents, Leslie and Russell Marsh. As the morning started to get away from her, she hoped to catch Marsh before he potentially left for work. It was a twenty-five-minute drive from the Crouse residence, having her pull into the Marsh driveway at 7:52.

It was a much smaller house than the Crouse residence, the type of house that had likely been built in the '70s or early '80s and had undergone absolute no modifications at all—not even a fresh coat of paint on the exterior. When she saw no cars in the driveway, she feared that she had missed her window of time, certain that no one would be home.

She went to the front door and knocked anyway. As she waited, she took in the sounds of a typical quiet morning in the DC suburbs: faraway engines, a murmur of industrial machinery somewhere, a dog barking, a car horn here and there. And somewhere among it all, there was a killer—if he wasn't, in fact, behind this door.

As if the thought had summoned someone, the door was answered. On the other side, she saw a young man of about twenty-one or so. He looked tired and a little confused. He was wearing a baggy Nirvana T-shirt and a pair of equally loose athletic shorts. His long black hair swept over his left eye and behind his neck.

"Are you Chris Marsh, by any chance?" Mackenzie asked.

"That's me," he said, now seemingly *very* confused. "Who's asking?"

She slowly took out her badge and gave her usual introduction. "Mackenzie White, with the FBI. I need you ask you a few questions."

His eyes went wide but she saw no fear there; it was complete confusion and maybe a bit of disbelief. "Well, um, this is my parents' house and they've already left for work, so…"

"Of course," she said. "Although, I know that you are at least twenty years old *and* you get your mail delivered here. So this is *your* place of residence and since you're not a minor, it's within the law for me to question you here."

She kept on a cheerful tone the entire time, trying to set him at ease. She'd love to get a much clearer picture of his mental state before she walked into the house. So far, from what she could tell, he had just woken up to having an FBI agent on his doorstep. He was understandably taken off guard and surprised.

"I guess come on in, then," he said. "I mean, what's going on? Am I in trouble or something?"

"No. But your name has come up in a case I'm working on and I'm hoping you can—"

"Oh my God," Chris said. "Is it Woodall? That killer guy got him?"

"That's a pretty great guess," Mackenzie said. "How'd you get there?"

"I heard about that Catholic priest. How he was crucified on the door to his church. And then that other one a few days ago...I saw that on the news yesterday. And...well...if my name came up and you're here...I'm assuming it's because of some nasty things I've shared recently. You've spoken to Mr. Crouse, I take it?"

"I have."

"Yeah, then come on in," he said, stepping aside.

Chris spent a few moments apologizing for the state of the place. His mom and dad had already left for work. Chris himself had not gone to college, he explained, and because he was between jobs, he was living in his parents' basement. He explained all of this as he sat down in a small recliner and Mackenzie settled in on one side of a small couch in the Marshes' living room.

"So what do you know about what's happened to me?" Chris asked.

"I know what you accused Pastor Woodall of. And I know that you confided in Mr. Crouse, showing him text messages and pictures. And please know that he did not give up that information easily. Quite frankly, he was a wreck when I left."

Chris shrugged. "I get it. In light of recent events, I understand why he'd offer up that information. But...I guess I don't get why you're here."

"For starters, I'd like to know your whereabouts last night."

Chris sat back hard in the recliner. He looked mortified in an instant. "What? You think I did it? That I've been the psycho nailing people to churches?"

"I think your name came up as the only person with a known grievance against the most recently deceased and it's my job to eliminate all possibilities."

After saying this, she watched another change flutter across Chris's face. He went from being mortified to angry and defensive. The shift in his eyes was nearly uncanny. "Well, that's pretty fucking offensive," he shouted. "I guess pinning gross murders on the kid that's been sexually abused makes sense since I have to be all kinds of fucked up, right?"

He was on his feet now, screaming at her. Mackenzie also got to her feet, very slowly. Something about the immediate shift in emotion raised alarms in her head. There might be some sort of mental issue here—an unknown factor that she had to treat with as much caution as she would if she suspected he was hiding a concealed weapon.

"Chris, I'm just here to ask some simple questions. And I'll only tell you one single time that responding in such a way is only going to make this worse for you."

"I'll tell you one thing," Chris said, trembling now and speaking much quieter. "I would have loved to kill him. It's a sin I've wrestled with for months. The things he did to me...the things he threatened..."

"Chris, let's just sit back down and talk this out."

"What's to talk about?" he asked. Again, there was a mood shift that came out of nowhere. He was screaming again. He took a step toward her, closing the distance between them to less than ten feet. "You think I killed him. That's why you're here, right?"

"Chris, you can't—"

He screamed so suddenly that Mackenzie's hand flinched down and to her right, ready to go for her Glock. She hesitated, though, a little embarrassed by her reaction. And maybe, in the end, it was that hesitation that made Chris think he had some sort of an opening.

He charged at her, lowering his head and squaring up his shoulders like he was a linebacker. It was a clumsy stance and he was being propelled by whatever strange and almost fugue-like anger she'd seen come across his face. Because of that, she easily blocked the attack. In doing so, she locked his head loosely with her right hand, grabbed his arm with her left, and threw him over in a makeshift hip toss. He landed half on and half off of the sofa, eventually falling to the floor.

Before he even had time to realize what had happened, Mackenzie was pulling his arms behind his back and slapping handcuffs on him. He screamed at her again, a sound of pure fury that seemed to dissolve as his shoulders and struggling legs started to give up the fight. He seemed out of sorts again; she imagined that another of those expression changes was taking place on his face as she hauled him to his feet.

"I didn't kill him," Chris said, whimpering now.

Mackenzie wheeled him around and looked him in the eyes, making no effort to hide her frustration. "Even if you didn't," she said, "you did just make a run at an FBI agent. So either way, you're headed to an interrogation room."

"But I don't—I don't know—"

She could see on his face that he was clearly confused. His eyes were wide and wandering, switching between fear, panic, and confusion.

Yeah, she thought. *There's got to be some sort of mental condition at work there. Maybe the trauma of the abuse at the hands of Woodall.*

Whatever the case, she still had to do her job. So she led him back through the door and to her car where she guided him into the back seat. By the time she had gotten behind the wheel, Chris Marsh was a blubbering mess in the back seat.

He made no attempt at conversation as she pulled out of the small driveway and into the street. But on the few occasions she looked into the rearview, she caught that same vacant look in his eyes—the desperate stare of someone who was lost and was only now discovering it.

CHAPTER ELEVEN

By ten o'clock, Mackenzie had allowed herself two cups of coffee. She downed them as she worked with Harrison and Yardley to pull together a complete work-up of the life and times of Chris Marsh. And it hadn't taken long for many of Mackenzie's assumptions to be proven correct.

From early childhood, Chris Marsh had suffered from severe attachment disorder, something he did not fully recover from until the age of twelve. Once the parents had been contacted and told that their son was currently being held by the FBI under suspicion of involvement in a murder case, the mother had been quite helpful in filling in the blanks. Chris had also been diagnosed with autism at a young age, but very low on the spectrum. By the time he was eight, the diagnosis had no longer held any sway.

Mackenzie and Yardley discussed this while Harrison was making calls to the leadership groups of Cornerstone Presbyterian and Blessed Heart to see if he could find any links between those churches and Chris Marsh. The more Mackenzie got to know Yardley, the more she liked her. She was a sharp agent, but maybe a bit naïve. Still, it was evident that she had no problem playing second fiddle, as long as she was learning something in the process.

"Okay, so what do the medical records say?" Mackenzie asked as they sat at a table adjacent to the interrogation room.

Yardley thumbed through a few pages sitting in front of her and shook her head. "He hasn't seen any doctor for more than two years. The last visit was for strep throat. The last recorded psych evaluation of any kind was when he was thirteen and the results look to be all right from what I can tell. We're having an expert check that right now."

Even if it's just a brief smattering of red flags in his psych history, there's no telling what Woodall's abuse brought back to him, Mackenzie thought. *Especially if he suffered from an attachment disorder as a young kid.*

She kept thinking of those mood switches, though. Something was certainly unhinged within the young man. To go from tired and accommodating to angry and defensive in less than ten minutes…that was pretty spectacular.

49

"Thanks for all of your help," Mackenzie said. "Can you try to speed the psych records evaluation up? And light a fire under Forensics, would you? I'm still waiting on results from the nails found at the earlier scenes."

Yardley nodded, eager to help. Mackenzie left the table and headed out toward the interrogation room. There was a single agent standing guard. When he saw Mackenzie coming his way, he nodded to her and took a set of keys out of his pocket. He unlocked the door to the interrogation room and let her in. When it slid closed quietly behind her, she saw that Chris Marsh looked to be in a docile state.

It was the first time she'd laid eyes on him since she'd pulled into the parking garage with him in tow. From there, he'd been escorted into the building by three other agents while Mackenzie had taken a few moments to update McGrath. She saw no glimmer of that fury in his eyes but that meant nothing to her—it had not been there when he had first answered the door at his parents' house, either.

"Do you think we can have a conversation now, Mr. Marsh?" she asked.

Chris nodded. "Yeah. Listen. I'm sorry as hell about earlier. I got freaked out and upset and I just...I don't know. I snapped."

"Does that happen often?"

"No. I get mad pretty easily, but never like that. But the last month or so, I've just felt like this giant ball of pent-up anger and frustration, waiting to go ballistic. And, well, you were the first person to tell me about Pastor Woodall. I hate him.. I really do. But at the same time, he was part of my life. Without him, I don't think I could have admitted it to myself."

"Admitted what?"

"That I'm gay. I think maybe I've always known. That's how I started meeting with him. Asking him to talk to me about it. And after a few months...well, we started things up."

"Was he abusive the entire time?" Mackenzie asked.

"No, not at all. But I think over time...maybe a few months or so, he started to realize what he was doing and what it might cost him. He'd tell me about it and I suggested that we just end it. He was much older and I did know the risks he was taking. But when I seriously started talking about it, *that's* when he'd get violent."

Mackenzie digested this, taking it all in while watching his face. Whatever had caused him to lash out at her several hours ago was gone. Something inside of him had broken in that time and she now found herself looking at a broken young man.

She was glad that the affair and the abuse itself had little relevance on the case. The idea of it made her cringe, made her see the recently deceased as a monster. So she did her best to push it aside without making Chris feel as if his trauma was not being belittled.

"Chris...did anyone other than Eric Crouse know about the affair?"

"No. I mean...who am I going to tell? I'm ashamed of it. Not the gay part...although my parents still don't know. But the affair. I mean...he had a wife. He had three kids, one of which is nearly my age."

"You're certain of this? You don't think Pastor Woodall maybe told someone?"

"I highly doubt that. He had everything to lose. He had absolutely no reasons to go public. Not to anyone. But I can't know for certain."

That's an extremely valid point, she thought.

"Chris, have you ever attended church services at Blessed Heart Catholic Church or Cornerstone Presbyterian?"

"No. My family has always gone to Living Word. My folks were pretty adamant about it. They liked it because it was nondenominational. Mom grew up as a Catholic and regrets every minute of it."

"And now let me go back to where I was trying to lead the conversation earlier," Mackenzie said. "It all goes back to you being the only name we're getting that would have a viable grudge against Pastor Woodall. I need to know where you were all night last night. Do you have proof of where you were?"

"My parents," he said. "I never even left the house last night. And most of the night, I was online, looking for jobs. I sent off a few emails and filled out a couple of forms. One of them was pretty close to midnight, I think. You're welcome to check out my computer for all of that proof."

She nodded, not wanting to tell him that there was likely already someone looking over the contents of his computer right now.

"Thank you," Mackenzie said. "I think that'll be all for now, Chris."

She got up to leave, but he stopped her pretty quickly. "Agent White? Can I ask you something?"

"Sure."

Chris seemed to choose his words very carefully before speaking. He would not meet her eyes as he asked the question, staring at his hands which were clasped in his lap.

"If he did this stuff with me—the sex and abuse, I mean—do you think I'm the only one? If there are other guys out there that he's messed with, I hate to think what they might be feeling. You know? There were times when I just wanted to kill myself."

A man of Woodall's age, with a huge congregation, who threatened and abused a boy out of fear of having a homosexual affair exposed, Mackenzie thought. *That's a damned good point. The chances of Chris being the first are slim to none.*

"I don't know," Mackenzie said. "But that's one of the things that we need to look into for sure."

As she left the interrogation room, something Chris had said in passing came back to her. It was an empty comment almost, one that most people would have just glossed over. But as she stood outside of the interrogation room, it now seemed pretty important. She had asked him if he had ever attended Blessed Heart or Cornerstone Presbyterian.

No, he'd said. And then he'd gone on to say: *My folks were pretty adamant about it. They liked it because it was nondenominational. Mom grew up as a Catholic and regrets every minute of it.*

There had to be a link between the three men who had been killed. Somewhere, there had to be some sort of connection. She'd heard of lapsed Catholics or people transitioning from Baptist to Lutheran and so forth. She also knew that it might be something of a culture shock for someone from a Presbyterian background to start attending a Catholic church.

But it happens, I'm sure, she thought. *And while it might take forever to try to find one person who attends Living Word who has also attended Blessed Heart or Cornerstone, it might not be quite as hard to find someone who* works *there who can give something of an inside view.*

She knew where she needed to go next. And even though she felt like her morning was on some sort of endless loop, she carried on. She said her goodbyes to Yardley and hurried to the parking garage, heading out to pay yet another visit to Eric Crouse.

CHAPTER TWELVE

Eric Crouse's wife was understandably not happy to see Mackenzie again. After all, the last time Mackenzie had visited, her husband had been reduced to a sobbing mess. She didn't even bother saying anything to Mackenzie when she answered the door. She simply walked away after giving Mackenzie a scowl, leaving the door open behind her. Having not been formally invited in, Mackenzie remained there on the stoop.

A few moments later, Eric came to the door. He looked much better than he had earlier that morning; he was more composed and looked to have gotten a great deal of grieving done in the hours that had passed.

"Agent White," he said, stepping out onto the stoop and closing the door behind him. Apparently, she would not be invited in this time.

"Sorry to bother you again, but in speaking with Chris Marsh, a thought occurred to me. And I'm hoping you could maybe point me in the right direction."

"I can certainly try," he said. "How *is* Chris, by the way?"

She elected not to tell him about how Chris had tried to attack her, possibly dealing with some sort of unresolved mental issues from the stress and trauma of his last few months. Instead, she settled for a half truth. "He's doing okay," she said. "He's obviously dealing with a lot but he was able to help as well as he could. But it occurred to me that my best bet at getting any kind of solid lead is going to be finding a connection between the churches or their leaders themselves. You, being a former elder at Living Word, I thought you could maybe help in that regard."

With his arms crossed, Eric nodded. "Well, a few things come to mind. First, there are often events or conferences here in DC. They also have them in northern Virginia and parts of Maryland. It's these events where speakers get together for leadership talks and sort of honing in on God's word. I know for a fact that Pastor Woodall and Father Costas have attended some of those together. They weren't friends or anything like that, but they were civil when around one another. There were always varying theological arguments between them but they were always very respectful."

"And what about Reverend Tuttle?" Mackenzie asked.

Eric shrugged. "I don't know him well. And at the risk of sounding like a snotty and spoiled man, you have to remember that Cornerstone Presbyterian is relatively small. Reverend Tuttle wasn't usually in on circuits like that—conferences and things of that nature."

"You said a few things come to mind," Mackenzie said. "What are some others?"

"Well, I'm just thinking about a guy that used to serve at Living Word. He might still be attending there...I honestly don't know. He served at the Welcome Center and helped out with the children's ministries. I don't recall his last name, but his first name is Greg. He's coming to mind because I know for a fact that he came to Living Word after leaving Cornerstone Presbyterian. I spoke to him a few times in passing on Sunday mornings. Part of his story is how people at Cornerstone found out about his past and kind of turned their backs on him. They never actually asked him to leave, but it was clear to him that's what they wanted."

"What sort of past?"

"I'm not sure. He was kind of vague about it. Again, these were just quick discussions in passing in the craziness of Sunday mornings at a pretty big church."

"When you say he *served*, what do you mean?"

"Well, he wasn't an employee of the church or anything like that. At Living Word, there are ministries for just about everything. And people within the church volunteer to help within those ministries. Greg was one of them."

"And even with a past that even he admitted is shady, he was able to serve?"

"Yes. At Living Word, they are very sincere about not judging people based on their pasts—just on the people they can be in the future with the help and love of Christ. Although, for the children's ministry, he'd have had to go through a background check. So if that came out fine, it eliminates a lot of criminal activity in his background."

"And was there any disagreement between him and Pastor Woodall?"

"Not really," Eric said. "I do recall a time after a sermon on forgiveness and reconciliation that Greg pulled me to the side after service and asked questions about the message. A few things Pastor Woodall said had rubbed Greg the wrong way. But I don't think there was anything mean about it. Just...sometimes the word of God can cut us, you know? But again, I repeat, I didn't really know the guy all that well. But I do know he has a solid connection to Cornerstone Presbyterian and he *has* told me that he left there because he felt he was being judged by his past."

"And you don't remember his full name?"

"No, I'm sorry," he said, pulling his phone from his jeans pocket. "But if you give me a second, I can probably get it for you."

He started typing up a text message and as he did so, Mackenzie took a moment to try to put the pieces Eric had just given her into the messy puzzle she had poured out in her head. This would be the first verifiable connection between one person who had history with both Living Word and Cornerstone. If by some strange coincidence this person was also familiar with Blessed Heart, there could be pay dirt.

Those chances are slim, though, she told herself. *And one guy with a checkered past who did some church bouncing because messages and attitudes were making him uncomfortable isn't all that uncommon. It certainly doesn't make him a suspect. But it* does *make him a potential resource for how the two churches could possibly be linked.*

The sound of Eric receiving an incoming text broke her concentration.

"Man, people are on the ball this morning," Eric said. "I guess tensions are high with what happened to Pastor Woodall. Anyway, I pinged a guy that is one of the leaders back in the children's ministry. He says the guy's name is Greg Yoder. And he no longer attends Living Word."

"Greg Yoder," Mackenzie said, committing it to memory before she typed it into a text message of her own for a request for more information from headquarters. "Thanks so much, Mr. Crouse."

She hurried back to her car, again reminded just how accustomed she had gotten to having Ellington at her side. Without him there to pull the occasional wisecrack or flirtatious comment, the morning seemed to be moving quite slow.

When she placed the request for Greg Yoder's contact information, it was only 11:40. But the day already felt like it had stretched on forever—and also like it didn't intend to speed up anytime soon.

That did, however, change slightly when she received a call from Harrison five minutes later.

"Mac, I think we might have something here," he said. "It turns out that Greg Yoder has a history that is incredibly relevant to your case. As a kid, he attended Blessed Heart. More than that, he was one of two teenagers who stepped forward with claims of abuse."

"At Blessed Heart? You're sure?"

"I'm looking at the police report right here on my laptop," he said. "The case was later dropped without any real reason given but yes…Greg Yoder accused a priest at Blessed Heart of sexual misconduct at the age of sixteen."

"I think you're right, Harrison. We just might have something after all. Yoder also has ties to both Cornerstone and Living Word."

"You need me or Yardley to come meet you?"

"No, I think I'm good. A man with a history of abuse from someone he saw as an authoritarian—he won't take kindly to being piled up on. Do you mind just sending me the address?"

"Absolutely. Good luck."

With that, she ended the call and waited on Harrison's text. She felt a familiar anxiousness creeping into her as she waited.

Maybe today would start speeding up after all.

CHAPTER THIRTEEN

The morning had crept along to the point where most everyone in the city was at work. This included Greg Yoder, who worked as a manager at a downtown FedEx office. Mackenzie pulled up in front of the building, situated in the center of a strip mall, and checked the information Harrison had sent her once again. Yoder was twenty-seven and currently enrolled in a local community college. He had no criminal record, his name only appearing in police reports for the hushed abuse scandal from eleven years ago.

When Mackenzie walked into the FedEx place, there were several people standing around, a few at the front counter while others looked around at the envelopes and stationery. Lunch rush, Mackenzie assumed as she stepped forward toward the counter.

When she got there, she saw three employees behind the counter. One of them was working on a project at a large printer off to the right. He was a tall, young-looking man. When he turned just slightly in Mackenzie's direction, she could read his name tag: **Greg**.

Mackenzie approached the counter, getting irritable looks from those waiting in line. The young girl behind the counter gave her a similar glare, looking from Mackenzie and then to the back of the line.

"Yeah, I know," Mackenzie said. "But I'm here to speak with the manager."

"He's busy at the moment," the girl said.

"I can see that," Mackenzie said, nodding at Greg, still by the printer. "But I assure you, this is urgent."

She was doing everything she could to not pull her badge and cause a scene. But if she had to, she would. Fortunately, something in her gaze must have unnerved the young girl behind the counter because she left her place at the register and went back to the printer. There, she whispered something into Greg's ear. Greg looked up toward Mackenzie, gave a confused look, and then left the printer.

"Can I help you?" he asked quickly as he approached the counter.

Mackenzie waited for the girl to resume her place at the register before answering, "I'm Agent White with the FBI, and I need to speak with you."

Greg gave her a look that indicated he clearly didn't believe her. Mackenzie leaned closer to him and looked him in the eyes. "I can pull my badge and show you, but I figured you wouldn't want your co-workers and customers to see. It's your call."

"There's an office in the back," he said rather quickly.

"Thank you. I won't use up too much of your time."

Greg was clearly frightened as he walked over to the girl at the register. "I know it's busy," he said, "but I need you to cover for me for a few minutes."

More irritated than ever, the girl nodded. Greg opened up a waist-high hinged door along the counter to allow Mackenzie behind it. He led her past a row of copiers and printers, into a small hallway hidden away from the rest of the store. The office he led her into was indeed small and smelled like someone's microwaved lunch.

Mackenzie closed the door behind them. There was a single desk and only one chair that neither of them used.

"You look nervous, Greg," she said.

"I've kind of been expecting someone to come talk to me. I figured just the police, though. Not the FBI."

"Why would the police come talk to you?"

"Well, Father Costas was murdered, right? Last I checked, the killer still hasn't been found. I figured with my complaint filed against him as a teenager, I'd eventually be sought out for questioning."

"How did you feel when you knew he was dead?"

"Honestly…my first thought was that karma is a bitch. If you want to know if I was sad about it, I'm not going to lie. That old bastard got what he deserved. I know it sounds harsh and very un-Christian, but…"

"Do you have any alibis for the night he was killed?"

"I stay over at my girlfriend's apartment most nights," he said. "She can vouch for me. If I'm not there, I'm at the library."

"You're going to community college, right?"

"Yeah. Getting a late start, I guess. But after I made those allegations against Father Costas, my life kind of went downhill. That damned story took up my entire life. I applied to colleges and had great grades. But no one would take me. The story about my allegations was never national news or anything, but I think it made the rounds enough to screw up my life for a few years."

"Tell me, Greg...have you heard about any other murders in the last few days?"

He shook his head. "I don't really watch the news. The only way I found out about Costas was from my mother calling to tell me."

"Well, there have been two more, and they were both leaders of churches. Churches I believe you attended and had some sort of issue with."

"What?" Greg asked, genuinely shocked. The word came out as little more than a gust of air.

"Reverend Tuttle of Cornerstone Presbyterian and, just last night, Pastor Robert Woodall at Living Word."

"Oh my God," Greg said, a trembling hand rising up to his mouth.

"You've attended those churches, correct? I have it on good authority that you even served on a greeting team and in children's ministry at Living Word on occasion."

"That's right," Greg said. "I...uh, I left Cornerstone because they were too hung up on my past. They apparently don't believe that someone can escape their past. The congregation there...they just wanted nothing to do with me. So I left and started attending Living Word."

"But you had issues there as well, right?" Mackenzie asked.

"No, nothing like I experienced at Cornerstone. It was just...I don't know. The messages were a little too liberal for me. It took me no time at all to figure out that they were very accepting of me and my past but there were other things they believed that I took issue with. The message sometimes made me very uncomfortable."

"Did you ever have direct conversations with Pastor Woodall?"

"Once. I went up to him after the service and asked him to go into greater detail about the grace that God extends to us."

"Did it lead to an argument?"

"Not at all."

Mackenzie weighed her options. She would of course check in on his alibis for the nights and mornings of the murders. But her gut was already telling her that Greg Yoder was not a killer. He was just an unfortunate man who was haunted by a past that it seemed like he might never escape.

"Let me ask you one last thing," Mackenzie said. "All those years ago, when things with Father Costas went down...was it a mutual thing?"

Greg looked at her like she had just slapped him. But when he saw no judgment in her face, he sighed and wiped a stray tear away.

"The first time he tried something, it was mutual. He was very complimentary and I was at that age where I was just curious, you know? But after a few seconds...I told him no. But he didn't like that. No one ever told him no, apparently. I remember him even saying one time, 'Do you want to know what happens to boys that tell me no?' It was twisted."

"And how many times did he abuse you?"

"Twice. The first time was brief because I ran out of there. But the second time...I figured it was okay. Just get it over with, you know? But then I met another kid who was going through the same thing and...well, we decided to go public. If it happened to us, surely it was happening to others, you know?"

Mackenzie nodded. She was feeling another lead slip away, but at the same time, other avenues within this case were starting to open up.

Alleged abuse with Costas at Blessed Heart. Alleged abuse with Woodall at Living Word. That means motive for someone and much more than a basic connection.

"I appreciate your time, Greg," she said.

"Sure. And with Woodall and Tuttle...were they killed the same way?"

"Yes, they were. So if you think of anyone who might have been able to carry out such an act or would even have any reason to, please let me know. Especially anyone you know who might have been abused by these men. What about the other young man that came forward with you?"

Greg frowned. "His family moved to Florida after it all went down. I got a call from his sister about a year later. He hung himself in his bedroom."

Mackenzie had almost been expecting such news but it still shocked her. She also did her best to view it as more than just a missed opportunity for another lead, but as a tragic loss of human life at the hands of deplorable abuse.

She handed Greg one of her business cards and opened the office door. "Thanks again for your time. And please do let me know if you can think of anyone else who might be able to help."

Greg only nodded as he pocketed the card. As Mackenzie left him in the office, it occurred to her that with each person she questioned about the case, she was uncovering scabs that had taken a while to form. And while she realized that questioning these people was essential to cracking the case, it made her feel no better.

It also made her determined to catch this bastard sooner rather than later so she could stop causing people pain by dredging up pasts that they were trying to forget.

With that, she figured she needed to start at the beginning. She thought of Father Costas and the ornate façade of Blessed Heart.

Abuse from eleven years ago and he was still the prominent figure within the church, she thought. *As far as I'm concerned, that means there's a cover-up somewhere.*

And that was a scar she didn't mind uncovering at all.

CHAPTER FOURTEEN

It was much harder setting up an appointment with the Cardinal's office than Mackenzie thought. In the end, she'd had to use her bureau sway. She knew that in doing so, there was no way they could deny her—especially with Costas's murder still in the forefront of the public's mind. She knew that it would be wishing for the moon to get an appointment with the Cardinal on such short notice, but she did manage to bully her way into an afternoon appointment with one of the auxiliary bishops.

In a rather ironic twist of fate, the auxiliary bishop she was meeting with, a man by the name of Barry Whitter, was scheduled to be at Blessed Heart that afternoon to speak with members of the congregation for words of encouragement and worship in the face of the death of Father Costas. His secretary had given Mackenzie fifteen minutes of his time, before he was to meet with an interim priest at the church.

It felt strange to Mackenzie as she walked back up the stairs to Blessed Heart. When she opened the doors and went inside, she felt like she was walking into a tomb. The place was silent and a nearly tangible feeling of mourning filled the air.

She walked into the sanctuary, down the aisle between the rows of gorgeous pews. In front of the sanctuary, Auxiliary Bishop Whitter was sitting in the first pew, as they had scheduled. He stood to greet her and Mackenzie could tell right away that the smile on his face was an extremely fake one. Every footstep and movement seemed to make a massive noise in the large, quiet, and beautifully decorated church.

He's not sure of my intentions, she thought. It was an expression she had seen hundreds of times. But for a man of his stature and with his schedule, he probably felt a little disrespected. Given the two stories of abuse at the hands of the church she had heard today, Mackenzie really didn't care.

Still, she had a role to play if she wanted Whitter's cooperation. She returned his fake smile with one of her own and extended her hand for a shake. "Thanks so much for your time," she said, taking a seat on the pew. "I know you're busy, so I'll make this quick."

"If I can help find who has been killing these men of God, I consider it time well spent," Whitter said.

"Well, finding links between all three leaders has been tricky," she said. "I have managed to find a few connections that didn't quite pan out. But the last person I spoke with had a history with all three churches. Unfortunately, he wasn't able to shine any light on a suspect, either. But it did bring up an interesting question—something that I hope might be able to uncover motive or even tracks to finding the killer."

"And what question is that?" Whitter asked.

"It's a question that I came to while speaking with a twenty-seven-year-old named Greg Yoder," she said. "Does that name mean anything to you?"

The look on his face told her that the name absolutely *did* mean something to him. Whitter looked as if he had just caught a whiff of something particularly foul.

"I don't see what that young man has to do with this," Whitter spat. "Unless he's a suspect in the killings."

"Far from it," she said. "The question I had for you is how priests with a checkered past are allowed to take such a position of authority. That is…after Yoder's allegations eleven years ago, how was it that Costas remained in such a position?"

"Because the allegations are *just that*. Allegations!"

"Yes, sir…I understand that. But with all due respect, such allegations aren't exactly rare in the Catholic Church. Also, I know that the case was dropped out of court and I'm going to assume there was some money or influence of some kind passed behind locked doors."

"Agent White, if this is why you called me here—to berate and insult my faith—"

"Far from it, sir. I mean no disrespect or insult. I am quite literally just offering up facts. Facts that I hope you can shed some light on. My hope is that by getting to the bottom of the abuse claims, I'll be able to establish a more direct approach to finding the killer."

"So let me make sure I'm understanding you correctly," Whitter said. "You're asking if there was some sort of cover-up? That maybe Father Costas *did* commit those heinous acts and the Church is somehow covering it up to save his reputation?"

"That's exactly right," she said.

"Then with all due respect, I'm going to ask you to leave. Granted, this is not my church but I believe I hold more sway here than you do."

63

"Bishop Whitter, surely you can see how sending me away in such a manner only makes the situation seem worse."

He stood up, insinuating that he wanted her to do the same. He looked pained as he chose his next words carefully. "And surely *you* can see that any attempts to make the Church or its congregation look bad would harm your career. We know politicians quite well. Probably some of your superiors, too."

"That sounds like a flimsy threat," Mackenzie said.

"Call it what you want."

"I just did. It was a threat. Which shows you're being defensive. The question, of course, is *why*."

"You can paint the picture however you choose," Whitter said. "But by buying into the allegations of two wounded teenage boys, you make the church out to be the bad guy."

Mackenzie smirked at him as she got to her feet. "Well, a correction there, sir. There's only one of those boys left. The second killed himself less than a year after the *alleged* abuse."

Mackenzie turned and walked away. Over her shoulder, she called out: "Should your faith finally lead you toward opening up on these matters and helping with my investigation, I hope you'll call the bureau right away."

Her voice echoed through the empty church in a way that made the final reverberation of it sound like a ghost. She hoped like hell it was a ghost that would haunt Whitter—possibly scaring him into opening up and telling the truth.

CHAPTER FIFTEEN

Mackenzie returned home a little earlier than usual. With no further leads and Forensics handling their end of things back at headquarters, there was literally nothing she could do other than dive deep into the files that had accumulated in regards to the murders over the past few days. She tended to concentrate better while at home, not distracted by the general busyness of offices and cubicle spaces at work.

Besides...her living room—hers and Ellington's—was much more conducive to studying than her boxed-in cubicle at work.

She was scanning through her phone as she sat down on her couch and kicked her shoes off. She got excited when she saw that an email from the Forensics department had come through but then frowned when she saw the brief message within the mail: *Nothing substantial. Sorry. Still, here are the data sheets.*

She spent the next five minutes sticking some leftovers in the microwave and booting up her laptop. She hooked her laptop up to her printer and printed out the data sheets from Forensics. As the documents printed out and she started eating her dinner, she glanced around the apartment, smiling at the presence of her things scattered here and there. She knew that it would take a while for the place to really feel like *theirs* rather than *his,* but she was excited to make it happen.

With the Forensics files printed out, Mackenzie added them to her growing pile. She ate reheated ziti and zipped on a beer while reading about each murder. She eyed the forensics material, hoping to find some clue about what kind of blunt instrument had been used to nail the victims to the doors but found nothing substantial. Tuttle's scene *did* turn up rogue hair fibers that turned out to be his wife's hair, a stray piece that had somehow clung to Tuttle's own hair.

She'd made it a little over halfway through her files when her phone rang. She saw Ellington's name and face on the display, answering it right away.

"Shouldn't you be on a plane right now?" she asked.

"That was the plan, yeah. But there's been another lead. And before you get too excited, the case seems to be getting further and further away from your dad. There's something going on here for sure, but I don't know what."

"What going on?" she asked.

"It looked like just a dead vagrant at first," he said. "But then another one showed up, killed in the same way. By the time the third one had showed up in the course of five days, that's when McGrath sent me out. Your buddy Kirk Peterson seems to think the staging of the bodies and the blatant headshots suggest a ritualistic sort of killing that echoes the way your dad and the more recent victim with the Barker Antiques business cards were killed. But even he says it's a flimsy theory."

"So where does that leave you?" she asked.

"I'm going to work with Peterson and the local PD down here to track down this one last lead. If there's nothing at the end of it, *then* I'll be back home."

"Okay," she said. "Be careful. In the meantime, I'm going to just walk around the apartment naked. And sleep all alone. Naked."

He sighed on the other end of the line. "You're evil."

"I've been called worse," she said. "Go. Get to work."

She ended the call with a smile on her face. While she still felt a little jilted by not being asked to go to Nebraska, she knew that it was a decision that made sense. That's why it was so easy for her to turn her attention back to the case files in front of her.

She found herself going back to Pastor Woodall's file, mainly because it was the most recent. She could still see the early morning scene at Living Word church, the already-grieving employees huddled behind the crime scene tape. She could still clearly see Dave Wylerman, the head of the music department, struggling to keep a surge of emotion in check as she spoke with him.

As she brought Wylerman to mind, a small nugget of their conversation seemed to roll like a marble down a chute and take center stage in her brain.

"He had just gotten back from a retreat a few days ago...this little getaway he takes twice a year. It's a really quiet little island off the coast of Florida."

She considered this for a moment and then opened up Google. She tried a variety of terms, searching for something that might uncover a bit more information. After just a few minutes, under the search terms *pastors retreat island Florida,* she found what she was looking for.

She discovered that there was a small island just two miles to the south of another Florida island, Cayo Costa, that she had never heard of before. This island was called Kepper's Cay and from what she could tell, it was privately owned by a retired priest who now lived in South Africa. The island, located on the western coast of Florida, was only two miles in length and less than a mile in width. It contained a dozen bungalows that were routinely rented out to religious leaders, specifically for retreats and conferences.

Still reading over some of the information, Mackenzie grabbed her phone. She did not have Dave Wylerman's number, so she elected to text Eric Crouse. She sent a short message that read: **Dave Wylerman said Woodall had just gotten back from a small retreat/vacation on an island in FL. Might that have been Kepper's Cay?**

While she waited for a response, she navigated to the Contact Us page on the small and somewhat vague Kepper's Cay website. She saved the number to her cell phone and as she was inputting it, she received a response to her text from Wylerman.

Yup. Twice a year. Pretty sure there are a few big-name pastors, priests, etc that go there. Hope this helps!

I think it just might, Mackenzie thought.

She called the number she had just saved into her phone. As she expected, due to the time (it was closing in on six in the evening), no one answered the phone. However, a recorded message gave her another number to call in case of emergencies. She jotted down this number and called right away.

It was answered on the third ring by a man with a high-pitched and cheerful voice. "Hello?"

"Yes, I need to speak to someone regarding policies about obtaining information about people staying on Kepper's Cay."

"Um...are you currently staying on the island?"

"No."

"I'm sorry, but this is an emergency-only line and—"

"My name is Mackenzie White and I'm a special agent with the FBI," she said. "I'm calling because a man who stayed there a week ago was murdered last night."

"Oh my goodness," the man said, the cheer now gone from his voice. "In that case, what can I help you with?"

"I'd like a list of the names of people who have stayed there within the last year," Mackenzie said. "Would that be possible?"

"I can make that happen," he said, "but it's a little sketchy."

"I understand," she said. She gave the man her badge number, as well as McGrath's name and contact information. When she was done with that, she added: "You're welcome to check on any of that if you want, but time is of the essence here."

"Well, it might be several hours before I can get you a list like that."

"Okay, well, tell me this—in what capacity do you work on the island?"

"General Manager of Operations and Maintenance," he said.

"Okay. Rather than a list, what about a few names? If I give you some names, do you think you'd remember them...whether or not they have been to Kepper's Cay recently?"

"Oh yes," he said. "I make a point to establish relationships with everyone who stays here."

"Good. How about Father Henry Costas, a priest out of DC?"

"Yes. Father Costas was here...oh, I guess it was probably about five months ago. I'm pretty sure he stayed for a week."

"One more, if you don't mind," Mackenzie said. "How about Reverend Ned Tuttle?"

"Yes indeed," the man said. "He was here with some type of leadership group for a conference we had back in March. I remember him quite clearly because he helped a few of my employees with a plumbing issue in one of the bungalows."

That's a pretty solid lead, she thought. *All three men have been on that island. Why? And what, exactly, goes on there?*

"And what about the retired priest who owns the island? Could you provide me with his name?"

"That's Father Mitchell," the man said.

"Is he an easy man to get on the phone?" she asked.

"No. However, your timing is pretty perfect. He's currently on the island. If you need to speak with him, I can try to arrange it."

"That would be helpful," Mackenzie said. "Can you perhaps call me back at this number when you've set it up?"

"Of course," the man said, although he sounded quite uncertain—maybe even a little nervous.

Mackenzie got off of the call, looking over the website for Kepper's Cay. She thought it was a strong lead, especially if she might be able to get some time with the man who owned the place. Of course, she'd have to get McGrath's permission, and that might be easier said than done.

Still, she had to try. Besides, the place was practically screaming that it had answers—that there were leads and clues buried in its golden sands. Even McGrath wouldn't be able to deny such a lead.

She called him up and told him about her discovery, including the conversation she'd just had on the phone. It took less than two minutes to convince him and within ten minutes, she was booking a flight to Florida.

CHAPTER SIXTEEN

For just a moment, Mackenzie felt like she was a little girl. She was standing at the end of a ferry, the ocean wind in her face. Tiny plumes of water brushed against the side of the ferry, sending gentle mists into her face. She closed her eyes against it, breathed in the salt water, and relished the warm air on her face. She breathed it in and, for just a handful of seconds, was nowhere.

There was no case. No nightmares about her dead father. No hateful memories of the Scarecrow Killer. Nothing.

Then, of course, she had to open her eyes. The world came crashing back into reality around her as the ferry pushed her on, closer to Kepper's Cay. The morning towed along behind her, and it had been a long one so far.

She had blissfully managed to sleep on the airplane—a direct flight from JFK to Tampa International Airport. She arrived just after eight in the morning, allowing her enough time to grab a coffee and breakfast in the airport before renting a car to drive a little farther down the coast.

For a while, she nearly allowed herself to feel like she was on vacation. She had never had the opportunity to travel very much and while in Tampa Bay, even without seeing the beach, she could feel the ocean in the air. Knowing that she'd be catching a small ferry from the coast out to Kepper's Cay made it all the more exciting.

She toyed with the idea of taking a picture of the ocean and the beach as she stepped onto the ferry. She figured it would be a nice way for Ellington to start off his day—a picture of her current location while he was toiling away in Nebraska. But for now, she thought she'd keep it to herself. Despite the exotic location and the sense of being on a mini-vacation, she had a job to do and wanted to keep every possible distraction away.

The scenery was more than enough distraction, after all.

And it only improved as the ferry got closer to the island. There were only eight other people on the ferry and as far as she knew, she was the only one who would be unloading at Kepper's Cay. The other passengers were headed to some of the other small islands speckling the ocean nearby.

She watched as the sea unfolded before her, the morning sun bouncing playfully off the waves. Ahead of them, Kepper's Cay came into view. She could see the entirety of the island and from a distance of about half a mile, it started to look like the outline of an island from one of those high-end vacation brochures or commercials that stole images from the Maldives or somewhere like Bora Bora.

When she stepped off of the ferry and onto the island's single loading dock, the weight of her job started to sink in. While appreciating the view was perfectly fine, she knew that she had a potentially big meeting with a man who was usually hard to get any time with.

She'd Googled Father Mitchell earlier that morning while waiting at her gate at JFK Airport. He'd been born into quite a lot of money, as his father had worked for an undisclosed company that had paved the way for a branch of computer science that went huge in the early '80s. His mother had also been born into money so when she died when Ronald Mitchell was only eleven, a huge sum of money had gone to him, locked away in a bank account until he turned eighteen. Mitchell had turned to God after the loss of his mother, becoming heavily involved in a Catholic church in his hometown of Albany, New York. Eventually, by the age of forty, he became a priest. He served as a priest in New York for nine years, then moved to Boston, where he had continued to serve as a priest but also became heavily involved with the community. He won just about any award and honor a priest can get, even getting an audience with the Pope in 2011.

He retired in 2014 at the age of sixty, as he had been one of the very vocal members of the Catholic Church who spoke vehemently against all of the child abuse scandals. He spent most of his time in South Africa, where he purchased a home in 2008, and a private residence on Kepper's Cay.

He was also famously secretive, staying out of the spotlight when it came to all things of a religious nature. The last time his name had been in the headlines was when he had contributed a sizeable chunk of money to hurricane relief when a massive storm had slammed into the Miami area a few years back.

That's why she was so surprised to see him standing at the end of the pier, waiting for her. He was dressed in a basic polo shirt and khaki shorts. His feet were bare and he had a skin tone that indicated he spent quite a bit of time in the sun. His hair was long, hanging into his eyes, which he brushed back as she approached him.

71

"Father Mitchell," she said. "Thank you so much for meeting with me."

Mitchell shrugged and led her off of the pier. "Well, it seems to me that this was just meant to be. I arrived here two days ago and am leaving in three days. For you to call and inquire about this place within that window...seems like more than coincidence."

"Regardless, I know how busy you can be..."

Mitchell waved this away. "I'm not the hotly sought after commodity that people think I am," he said. "Now, how can I help you? Maybe a tour of the place first? It's such a beautiful day; it would be a shame to not enjoy some of the beach while you're here, don't you agree?"

What the hell, she thought. *No one has to know.*

With that, she kicked off her shoes. She was wearing a white button-down shirt and a pair of black pants—not necessarily beach-ready attire but still not unbearably uncomfortable. With her shoes off and her toes in the soft, warm sand she followed Mitchell away from the pier and directly to the right where they joined the beach. They walked along the edge of the water as she scanned the area ahead.

The beach was pristine, the sand golden and unmarred by litter. The bungalows and buildings were located off of the beach, though some of the bungalows were within fifty yards or so of the water. They were all situated among gorgeous landscaping that was decorated to resemble some dreamlike exotic locale. The place really was gorgeous, making her reason for being there seem almost abstract in a way.

"I assume," Mitchell said, "that your visit here has something to do with Father Costas. I heard about his death three days ago. I understand there's been another death very recently as well. Pastor Woodall, also from Washington, DC. Is that correct?"

"That's right," she said. "There's also been a third one—the reverend of a Presbyterian church. So naturally, this is now being viewed as a serial case. And as of now, we have no clues, no evidence, and no real leads. I was drawn to Kepper's Cay because all three of the victims have visited here in the last year or so."

"Yes, that's what I was told by Michael, the man you spoke with on the phone. I've got all of the paperwork on the three victims back at the main office, waiting for you."

"Father Mitchell, how many people typically stay here within the course of a year?"

"It varies. But the last three years, we've averaged around three hundred people. That's not including another two hundred or so that

72

come just to attend a conference or group retreat. Of course, we have records and names for everyone who has ever rented a bungalow here, but most reservations are paid for by either a church treasury office or a leader of the church."

"So in other words, there would be no way to easily weed out who might be the next victim simply based off of a list."

"I suppose that depends on how many agents you have to check a list and then contact all of the names on there," Mitchell said.

He continued to show her around the island, explaining the purpose of the place. As he pointed out their small conference center and the little chapel behind the bungalows, he explained that he reserved the island only for religious leaders and their efforts toward growing the church because he was becoming very aware of increasing oppression against the church in just about every corner of the world.

"It's one of the reasons I retired so early," he said. "People far away from God, ironically, want to blame His people when things go bad. And when all of the sexual abuse allegations tore through the Catholic Church in the late nineties, I saw the beginning of the end. Because of all of the media attention, I knew I could not properly serve God from a position of priesthood any longer. So I opened this island up to those men of God who might be feeling the same discouragement.

"Over time, word got out and I also allowed a few conferences to be held here. During peak times, there's a two-month waiting list. But still, this has become a place of rest and restoration for men of God and those close to them."

"Is there a set rate or does it change according to who is coming?" Mackenzie asked. "I ask only because Father Costas and Pastor Woodall were leaders of large churches that could certainly afford it. But Reverend Tuttle belonged to a smaller church. I'd imagine he would struggle to find the funds to book a place like this unless there was some sketchy business with offerings from the church."

"I obviously can't speak to that," Father Mitchell said. "But I *can* tell you that Tuttle *did* rent out one of our less expensive bungalows. And we did offer him a discounted rate. We knew he was from a smaller church, but we don't discriminate here. You don't have to be part of a mega church to enjoy the solitude we have to offer."

He led her further down the beach, to a wooden walkway that was bordered along the edges by all kinds of plants and flowers.

The walkway became a bridge that rose up over a small stream that led off to the left, heading back out to the beach.

Ahead of them, the only building that looked the tiniest bit out of place waited for them. It was clear that this was the central office. While it did boast some island décor on the outside, there was something quite formal about the structure of the building, as well as its placement away from all of the other buildings.

Mitchell led her inside to an empty room. The hum of an air conditioner filled the place but there was nothing else going on. He took her down a small hallway that dead-ended at a conference room. There, he pulled a seat out for her and gestured to a few stacks of paper sitting in the center.

"That's everything I have as far as records go for Costas, Tuttle, and Woodall," Mitchell said. "I'm afraid it's not much, but perhaps you can find some other links."

"This is great," Mackenzie said, legitimately meaning it. She couldn't have asked for more material or cooperation.

"I'll leave you to it, then," Mitchell said. "In the meantime, is there anything I can get you?"

"Maybe just a water?" she asked.

"Coming right up."

He left her alone and she instantly pulled the stacks of paper to her. There wasn't much—perhaps twenty-five sheets of paper in all. Most of it was financial sheets, showing where they had all paid, as well as the dates of their stays. From the information on the sheets, she saw that Father Costas had been coming to Kepper's Cay the longest; his first stay had been in 2010 and he had made eight visits since, including one for a conference on spiritual warfare.

Tuttle had only been once, visiting the island seven months ago. He'd stayed for three days and then left. She hated to seem so stereotypical, but she kept getting tripped up by the fact that the reverend of a smaller church had been able to afford to come to a place like this. It made her wonder what kind of issues had made Tuttle even need a retreat in the first place.

Hanging on that thought, she pulled out her phone and sent a text to Harrison. **Can you do some digging to see what sort of problems/issues Tuttle might have either been enduring or coming out of about 8-9 months ago?**

As she sent the text, Mitchell came back into the room. He was carrying a tall glass of water for her. A single wedge of lime bounced along the top. He offered it to her with a smile.

"Thanks," she said. "Hey, so I have a question for you. An awkward one, maybe. But I was wondering if there was some kind

74

of a running theme in the issues that bring people here. What sort of things are they seeking rest and solitude from?"

"Are you a believer?" Mitchell asked.

The question took her aback. It seemed to be a question that she was being faced with a lot lately. She sighed and said, "I suppose you could say I'm in the undecided category. Why do you ask?"

"I think to understand the stress these men face on a daily basis, you need to understand the responsibilities they shoulder. Leading people closer to a God that they very badly want to be in sync with. Serving as a sounding board for people's sins and darkest thoughts. And knowing all the while that they are held to a very high standard. It can be exhausting—physically, mentally, *and* spiritually."

"Would you ever offer the island to a leader you know for a fact has been involved in something wrong? Something criminal?"

"No. But then again, *I* would have to know it for certain. Very rarely do I take the word of news programs or tabloids."

She could tell that he knew where she was going. Being a former priest, surely he was more than familiar with the cases of child molestation and sexual abuse. So she left it at that, not wanting to anger him. They were on the same page and did not need to go any deeper.

"Anything else?" he asked.

"No, thank you."

Mitchell did not leave, though. He thought about something for a while and then took a seat at the table.

"Is it a link between them?" he asked. "Abuse?"

"Only for two of them," she said.

"I knew that Father Costas had been accused of it but there was never any evidence…not enough to sway my opinion of him, anyway. He was a good man."

"I'm not sure about the allegations myself," she said.

"If you truly think it's a link that can help you find the killer, I think I might know of a place you can start looking."

Mitchell looked saddened that he was even considering this avenue. But at the same time, Mackenzie could tell that he was troubled by something—perhaps something that dragged down his spirits more than he cared to admit.

"Father Mitchell?"

"I'm fine," he said. "It's just that I know for a fact that sexual abuse and molestation *does* happen within the church. Although the vast majority of allegations and accusations are false and made up

75

just to seek attention or money, I know that it *does* happen. And as proof of that, all you need to see is one of the recovery groups."

"Recovery groups?" Mackenzie asked.

"For victims of abuse at the hands of the church. As you can imagine, it's a group filled with unbearable shame, so the meetings don't get much advertising or publicity. Sort of like self-help groups, but hidden away in the corner."

"And why are you telling me about this?" she asked.

"Because there's one meeting in your neck of the woods on Thursday in Alexandria, Virginia. It's a group that meets three times a year. There are more than thirty groups in the country. I always get invitations to them because I was so outspoken against the

Church when the abuse scandals were rocking the headlines a while back."

"Will you be attending the one in Alexandria?"

"No. I haven't attended anything like that in about three years now. God forgive me, it wrecks me too much. It just about makes me lose my faith. But if your killer hasn't been caught before that meeting comes around, I'd highly suggest you check it out. It's Thursday afternoon at five o'clock. I'm not sure where yet, but if you'll leave your contact information with me, I'll let you know."

"Thank you," she said.

With that, Mitchell left the room once again. Mackenzie went back to the documents, finding very little to connect the three men. There was evidence that both Costas and Woodall had come on several occasions and that they had attended at least one conference each. But from what she could tell, they had not attended the same conference. Also, none of the three men had ever been on Kepper's Cay at the same time.

By the time she reached the final page, Mackenzie knew that there was nothing to link the men in the stacks of paper. Still, she felt that she had made *some* progress.

If nothing else, this proves that the men likely aren't linked other than their professions. Also, the information about the meeting for the survivors of abuse seems like it could be a potentially great resource. Plus...I got to visit the beach for a few hours.

She took a few photographs with her phone of the documents that showed the dates when all three men had been on the island. If nothing else, it provided something of a timeline and might come in handy when Harrison got back to her with that information on Tuttle.

As she was about to head out of the office to locate Father Mitchell, her phone rang. When she saw Ellington's name and face, she grinned. Maybe she'd get to rub his face in her little beach excursion after all.

"You home yet?" she asked.

"No," he said. She could tell right away from the tone of his voice that he wasn't in the best of moods. "Where are you right now?"

"You wouldn't believe me if I told you."

"Well, wherever you are, you need to book the soonest flight you can to Nebraska."

"What? Ellington…what's going on?"

"We're closing in on a lead. I've already talked to McGrath. I want you here, Mac. I think you need to be on this at this point."

"Yeah, okay," she said. Her brain desperately tried to switch gears but there was a hiccup in there somewhere.

Dead priests and pastors…sunny Florida beaches…now out to Nebraska…

She suddenly felt like she was being sucked up into a whirlwind.

"Mac?"

"I'm here. Just…taken off guard. Give me a few minutes. I'll book a flight and let you know when I'll be there. Ellington, is everything okay?"

"Yes, everything is good. We had a break, though. And this might…well, it might provide all the answers you've been looking for."

She looked dumbly down at the documents on Mitchell's conference room table. They seemed like artifacts from a different world. The entire case seemed insignificant now—a dangerous thought for an FBI agent for sure.

But suddenly, all she could think about was her father.

And she could not get away from this idyllic island fast enough.

CHAPTER SEVENTEEN

He loved God, he loved his church and he loved the people of his church. But man, oh man, did he hate sitting in the confessional booth.

Wade Coyle arched his back and checked his watch. It was 7:05. Technically, he could have left for home five minutes ago. But he knew that some people liked to straggle in a little late, in a rush to confess their sins either directly before or after dinner with their families.

Of all of his duties as a priest, taking confession was the only part he truly did not like. He'd heard some deplorable things behind his screen and the worst part of it was that he could recognize voices some of the time. He could place a face with the voice and, as a result, knew which of the men in the pews during service had confessed to downloading pre-teen pornography or which of the older women had allowed their daughter's boyfriend to touch her inappropriately.

Still, he understood the importance of the act—not just for his church but for each and every one of the people who came to him, sitting on the other side of that screen to unburden their hearts.

Still…if no one else showed up in the next ten minutes, he was leaving. Another priest was due to come occupy the booth at eight o'clock anyway.

No sooner had he made this promise to himself than he heard the little door on the outside of the confessional open up. He then heard the four footsteps that led to the chair in front of the screen and the slight creaking of the chair as someone's weight was applied to it. And then came the seven words that, to Father Coyle, had become almost cliché.

"Forgive me, Father, for I have sinned."

"And what sin would you like to confess today?" Coyle asked.

"I'm…well, I'm not sure, exactly. I think maybe it's idolatry. But it involves violence, too."

"Tell me about each one," Coyle said. Honestly, he was just phoning it in at this point. He found himself seeing if he could identify a face that went with the voice but was coming up with a blank.

Thank goodness for that, he thought.

"Well, I find myself adoring people of the world over God," the man said. "I know that I should seek my peace and solace from God, but…I suppose it's easier to trust and worship things I can see. People. Flesh. I look up to them and I glorify people rather than God. Is that bad?"

"Not if you're realizing it first," Coyle said. "Tell me…are these people you are idolizing celebrities or people you see every day?"

"I'm afraid it's not quite as easy as that. They aren't celebrities, that's for sure. But at the same time, they tend to be people with a bit of power and reverence to them."

"And how are you idolizing them?"

"It started out as just plain old envy," the man on the other side of the screen said. "But that became something worse. Something nastier. I saw them as God. As Mother Mary. As Christ. I wanted to worship them…to glorify them."

"Yes, that could be an issue. About the violence, though…are the two tied together in any way?"

"I don't know," the man said. "But I know when I see their blood, it makes me feel whole. It makes me feel like I have done something right."

"Blood?" Coyle said. His heart surged in his chest and his own blood went cold.

"Yes, Father. I have to spill their blood for them to be shown for the men they truly are. Whole. Pure. Strictly of God."

"My son…I'm afraid I don't understand."

There was no response.

Instantly, the news of the three deaths went through Coyle's mind. Costas, Tuttle, and that liberal pastor, Woodall.

"Son, are you—"

That's when a thunderous force shook against the confessional. The door on Coyle's side buckled and came snapping in. It was a puny sound, like kindling popping over a fire. He was so frightened by the attack on the door that it took him a moment to realize that there was a man behind it, stepping into the space on his side of the booth.

"I've been idolizing you, too, Father," the man said. "I'm sorry. But really…you deserve it. You deserve the glory…"

Before Coyle could open his mouth to protest, the man pummeled him with a hard right hand. Coyle saw for one brief moment that there was something in his hand, maybe a roll of

79

quarters or some sort of tool. Whatever it was, it made the punch feel like he had been hit in the face with a baseball bat.

Father Coyle went flailing against the side of the confessional as black stars zoomed across his field of vision. His stomach lurched and his head exploded with pain.

He saw the man's hand drawing back again, but, blessed be to God, he blacked out before he could feel its savage impact.

CHAPTER EIGHTEEN

Mackenzie sees herself standing in front of the house she grew up in. She walks up the porch stairs and sees a group of ravens huddled on the porch. As she shoos them away, she sees that one of them is wearing a crucifix around its black neck. It caws at her as she steps into the house and as she closes the door, she hears the ravens take flight behind them.

She steps into the house and there is her mother, asleep on the couch. The house is cast in darkness, the only light coming from the glow of the television, which is showing a late night talk show. The host says nothing, just stares dumbly out of the screen as if waiting for Mackenzie to start the conversation.

She walks past the television and into the kitchen. She tries flipping on the kitchen light but the lights do not respond. She looks back to the living room and sees that her mother is no longer there. The front door is open again and she can hear the ravens moving on the boards, apparently having come back to roost.

She turns back around and looks down the hallway. It is longer than the actual real-life version of it, stretching on for a seemingly impossible distance. She starts walking and as she does, she reaches for her Glock.

But instead of a firearm, she finds a Bible waiting there. Only, where the words HOLY BIBLE are typically stamped in gold or silver, hers says BARKER ANTIQUES.

She holds it in front of her, tight to her chest, and the pages start to fall out. As each one hits the floor, it sounds like a voice whispering to her.

"Get out of here."

"Go away."

"Get over this."

"Turn around."

She ignores them all and continues on. And when she finally comes to the end of the hallway, the Bible having rained its pages on her way down, she finds herself staring at her parents' bedroom door. She knows what is waiting for her on the other side. She knows what she is going to see but she pushes it open anyway.

Things are different this time. Instead of a bed, there is a cross. Her father hangs on it, and he is still alive. He leers down at her in a grimace of pain.

"Get me down, please..."

Mackenzie drops the Bible and turns to run back toward the living room. But there stands her mother, blocking the way. She is holding a sledgehammer and a ridiculously large nail. She smiles at Mackenzie and when she opens her mouth to say something, it is only the cawing of a raven.

Mackenzie opens her mouth to scream just as her mother drives the huge nail forward, directly for her throat, a scream that does not sound like her but rather the roaring of some huge engine that is pushing the world along on its insane rotation.

***

She jerked awake, realizing that the engine noise belonged to the plane she was currently on. She breathed deeply, suppressing the shudders that passed through her. She had to remind herself where she was—not in the bedroom her parents had once shared, but sitting in an airplane, headed back to the state where that damned house sat.

When her plane taxied in, Mackenzie checked her phone. As the Wi-Fi connection was made with the airport, her phone lit up with notifications. The sheer number of them was overwhelming but she did her best to catch up as the plane rolled to a stop before passengers could get off. She had two text messages from Ellington, one from Harrison, a voicemail from Yardley, and eleven new emails.

She went through them in order of importance. Both of Ellington's texts were to let her know that if he could not be at the airport, one of the local agents would be there to pick her up. Harrison's message was in response to the text she had sent him earlier, letting her know that there was nothing on public record to indicate that Reverend Tuttle had been through any major hardships of any kind over the last year or so. She then checked Yardley's voice message. She found it a little odd and, maybe, just a little disrespectful.

"Hey," Yardley said. "Look, McGrath has me in charge of this religious leader deaths case while you're in Nebraska. If you could give me a call to debrief me on your little day trip to Florida, I'd appreciate it."

She didn't bother responding to any of the messages, as passengers were being allowed to take their belongings from their overhead bins. Mackenzie was very aware that she was still in the same outfit she'd been wearing when she'd stepped off the ferry ten hours ago. She could even still feel little grains of sand in her shoes. As trivial as it seemed, she wished she had at least one change of clothes with her. As it was, though, she only had her laptop bag, bureau credentials, and nothing else.

She got off of the plane quickly. Now that she was on the ground and moments away from meeting up with Ellington, it seemed real now. It was more than just a possibility, more than just a dream—which it had seemed like when she had been in the air. She also wanted to get to work as quickly as possible so the case in DC did not dry up in her mind. She was still quite surprised that McGrath had okayed this sudden trip to Nebraska, especially on the heels of her trip to Florida. But she wasn't about to question it.

When she entered the airport through her gate, she was relieved to see that Ellington was there after all. He looked tired and a little flustered but the smile he showed her when she stepped toward him was genuine. They greeted one another with a kiss and a brief hug, as if they'd been doing it forever.

"I don't know which to be more confused about," Mackenzie said. "The fact that I'm all of a sudden wanted on this case or that McGrath gave me permission for it."

"No need to be confused," he said. "Just come with me. We're due at the Omaha field office in half an hour. I'll fill you in on the way."

They hurried through the airport, not being slowed down by any lines since Mackenzie had no bags. Ellington led her out and into the closest parking garage where they got into his rental. After he cranked the ignition, Mackenzie held her hand out in a *hold on* gesture. She then leaned in and kissed him deeply, in a way that would have been awkward in the airport.

"Okay," she said. "Now you can catch me up."

Ellington smiled and said, "Hold on. Let me catch my breath first."

***

As they skirted along the freeway and then took an exit down onto the highway, Ellington spent most of the time talking. He filled her in with the attention to detail of an experienced agent but with the demeanor of a man who was beginning to fall in love with her.

"I was called out because Kirk Peterson had convinced some FBI agents that the vagrant murders were pretty much identical to the murders of your father and the newer guy from a few months back. The thing is, there was absolutely *zero* evidence to back it up. That's why McGrath chose to send me out here. Without any solid leads or evidence, we didn't want to pull you away from the current case—or get your hopes up on your father's case.

"Not too long after I called you the first time to tell you there was really nothing to see out here, another body was discovered. This one had a certain business card tucked into his back pocket."

"Barker Antiques," she said.

"Bingo. The guy was a junkie, shot in the back of the head from point-blank range by a low-caliber gun. Same old same old, just like the other vagrants. But this time, there was a clue left behind. A smudge on the business card. It was a fingerprint, but only a partial. It was at that point that I called you. Since then, the guys in Forensics at the Omaha field office have been working with a records database to narrow down the search. I got a phone call just as I was stepping into the airport to meet you. They got a match. And this is a guy with a pretty terrible history."

"So what's being done right now?" she asked.

"Well, this guy's record is ripe. He's got two domestic abuse charges, petty theft, and then he just got out of prison two months ago after serving five years for conspiring to murder. So there's a task force being assembled. We've got his address. And we've got someone sitting outside of his apartment right now. If he leaves and heads somewhere else, we'll have eyes on him."

"And they want me in on this?"

"They didn't have a choice," Ellington said. "I insisted on it. And McGrath took my side. Everyone involved on this knows the connection to your father's murder. You won't be taking the lead, but you'll be completely hands-on if an arrest is made. If this thing comes to a close, you're going to be a part of it. Besides…even McGrath realized that no one knows more about the murders and the whole Barker Antiques ordeal than you. It just made sense to have you come in."

"Are we headed there now?" she asked.

"We're heading to the field office and then probably leaving there right away. If all goes well, this whole thing could be wrapped up within an hour or two."

"And to think," Mackenzie said, "I was walking along a beach nine hours ago."

"Yeah, you'll need to let me in on the secret of how in the hell you got McGrath to sign off on that."

"I think it paid off, though. The little retreat they have on that island checks out, as does the guy who runs it. But he gave me information that I think might work itself out into a considerable lead—or a very promising resource at the least."

"You're quite the seasoned traveler today," Ellington commented. "Are you sure you're up for this?"

"Absolutely," she said. "I just wish I had a change of clothes. Or at least time for a shower."

He smiled at her and said, "If we wrap this thing up, I'll see to it that you get a shower. And maybe, if you don't mind, I can lend a hand?"

"Let's see how this plays out first."

She appreciated the gesture and sentiment, but as they raced closer to the field office, Mackenzie started to get anxious.

Is this really it? she wondered. *Is this the day I get the answers I've been looking for when it comes to my father's death?*

Dusk settled in around Omaha as her nerves started to fire up. Every part of her knew that something big was moments away but she still found it hard to believe that it had fallen in her lap so easily.

***

Ellington hadn't been exaggerating. The moment Mackenzie stepped into the Omaha field office, she was approached by a man wearing a simple black suit and carrying a padded file in his right hand. He looked on edge, as if he were about to jump out of his skin in anticipation of getting things underway. His thick black hair was in disarray. He stood a little over six feet tall and had the composure of a man who looked like he was *always* motivated, on the move to get something done.

"Agent White, I'm Darren Penbrook, the lead on this case. I'm glad to have you on board. Has Agent Ellington debriefed you?"

"He has," she said. "I certainly appreciate you letting me come along on this."

"Of course, of course," Penbrook said, as if he really couldn't care less. Behind him, the central room of the field office was aflutter with activity. She saw two agents studying a map of the city on the wall behind a bullpen-like area.

"We're rolling out in exactly five minutes," Penbrook said, waving her and Ellington to follow him farther back into the building. "It'll be the three of us and two other agents. Your friend Kirk Peterson requested to come along but we denied it. There's just too much risk here."

"Are we assuming the suspect is dangerous?"

"The suspect is one Gabriel Hambry. In addition to the abuse charges and conspiring to murder marks on his record, he's also been the suspect in two different instances of suspected arms trafficking across the border into Mexico. We've never been able to pin it on him but all of the evidence points at him. And if that's the case, then yes—we're assuming he's heavily armed. And when the FBI comes knocking on his door…"

"I follow you," Mackenzie said.

Penbrook led them into a small room in the back. There, another man was on the phone, pinching it between his ear and shoulder so that he could properly cinch a holster onto his belt. The holster carried a Sig 357 semiautomatic. Seeing it made Mackenzie that much more aware of her own firearm holstered at her side, a Glock 22 that she had come to be all too familiar with.

The man ended his call and pocketed the phone. He held out his hand for a shake and introduced himself.

"Mark O'Doul," he said. "Good to meet you." He then looked at Penbrook and nodded. "Suspect is still in his apartment. Watching TV, it seems like."

"Good," Penbrook said. "Agent White, O'Doul will be accompanying us and taking the lead as we roll in. I understand that you have something of a personal attachment to this case but I ask that you let O'Doul and I handle the tactical side. Once we get Hambry into custody, you have my word that you get first crack at interrogation. And, you know…if he happens to make a run for it and pursuit ensues…maybe I turn a blind eye if you happen to get a little rough."

Mackenzie grinned and nodded, knowing better than to give any type of verbal cue to such a comment.

"Any questions?" Penbrook asked.

"How far away is Hambry's apartment?" Mackenzie asked.

"About half an hour, out in Plattsmouth," Penbrook answered. "O'Doul and I will take the lead in our car while you two follow. Our surveillance says we're going to be best positioned by parking on the street on the other side of the block. Gives us the best shot of coming up on Hambry's residence without giving him any sort of warning."

Plattsmouth, Mackenzie thought. While she had only ever passed through Plattsmouth while living in Nebraska, simply

86

hearing the name of the town made her feel as if she had come full circle—not that she had returned home by any means, but that she had revisited some ghost from her past that seemed to have been waiting for her forever.

"We have a warrant yet?" Ellington asked.

"Got it about three hours ago. Given the nature of our visit to Mr. Hambry, we won't exactly be knocking on his door. We'll be busting it down."

It was a bit juvenile, sure, but that closing comment from Penbrook got Mackenzie more excited than ever. She was moments away from nailing down the most promising lead in discovering what really happened to her father.

As far as she was concerned, the busting down of doors by force seemed fitting.

CHAPTER NINETEEN

Hambry's apartment was in one of those packed out apartment complexes that look like a carbon copy of any other building in the city. It was the kind of apartment complex you saw everywhere in the nation: plain, a little grungy, and very much average. Being a little after ten o'clock on a week night, they all assumed that the chances were quite good that Hambry was home.

Mackenzie and Ellington met Penbrook and O'Doul at the central walkway along the first floor. The night was quiet and it seemed that there was not a soul stirring anywhere within the complex. Far off in the distance, a man was walking his dog. Near the back of the building a woman was laughing about something. It was any other ordinary night. Mackenzie tried to remind herself of that. It was far too easy to get excited about what the next hour could hold. So to remind herself that it was just another routine part of her job to do what they were about to do would usually center her.

But not this time. In that moment, standing with the other three agents, she felt like so much of her career was hinged on what was about to go down.

"Hambry is apartment number three hundred and six," Penbrook said. "O'Doul and I will go in first. I want the two of you to wait three seconds and then file in behind us. If we do it right, it's a simple arrest. In and out and back to the office. Questions?"

Ellington shook his head. Mackenzie did the same, although in her head she was practically shouting at Penbrook to get the damned show on the road already.

Perhaps sensing her anticipation, Penbrook started down the walkway that led to the first flight of stairs. The stairs were simple, with no covering or carpet of any kind. Their footfalls thudded in hollow echoes, like little tiny taps of bass from a passing car stereo. They advanced somewhere between a fast walk and a sprint as they came off of the stairs on the third floor.

They stayed tight against the wall as they hurried down the open corridor. The street lights from below illuminated their way, their shadows following them as, one by one, they reached for their guns.

O'Doul brought them to a halt by raising his hand. All four of them were positioned against the wall between apartments 305 and 306. O'Doul waited a beat while standing by the frame to Hambry's door. He then held up three fingers. Mackenzie watched as those fingers dropped one by one, counting down to the moment they would burst through the door.

Three…two…one.

With nearly spring-loaded motion, O'Doul took one step away from the wall, pivoted, and then raised his foot. He delivered a solid kick that suggested he had done this more than a few times. Even without being able to see the result, Mackenzie knew the door had snapped open. She watched as O'Doul and Penbrook filed in one behind the other. Ellington turned to her, silently counted to three, and then they followed in as well.

Mackenzie entered with her Glock aimed level and to the left, completing the fanned-out alignment the other three agents had begun.

But she did not stay situated that way for long.

The sight before her was simply too bizarre. It was difficult to hold her composure as she looked into the living room, which the apartment door led into.

A man sat in a recliner, giving them a view from the side. He was not moving. Not only that, but the recliner was soaked in blood. Splatters of it were also all over the wall. Mackenzie stepped forward. She knew she might be overstepping her bounds, but she stepped in front of Penbrook, sidling up next to O'Doul. As she angled herself to get a better look at the man, she was dimly aware of Ellington and Penbrook inching further into the apartment to check the other rooms.

Mackenzie was now standing directly in front of the man. From the brief file she had seen on Gabriel Hambry at the Omaha field office, there was no question that this was him. And as she stood directly in front of him, looking at him, the situation only got worse.

Hambry had been shot in the back of the head. Without a close study, Mackenzie was pretty sure it had been from a smaller caliber weapon. Still, at point-blank range, it had done some messy work.

But honestly, she wasn't looking too closely at the gunshot wound or the gore that it had caused. She was more interested in the item that had been affixed to Hambry's shirt with a safety pin.

It was a business card.

Blood had splattered along most of it, but it was easy to see the business name printed on the front.

Barker Antiques.

"What the hell?" O'Doul whispered from beside her.

"Whoever it is, he's playing with us," Mackenzie said. She very badly wanted to be mad, to be filled with rage at having had her face rubbed in this mess. But instead, as much as she hated to admit it, she was actually rather scared.

Ellington and Penbrook came back into the living room. Ellington wasted no time in coming over to her when he saw the look of shock and confusion on her face. He let out a very pronounced curse when he saw the situation for himself.

"So Hambry was just a pawn, then?" Penbrook asked.

"Looks like it," Mackenzie said. She wanted to tear the business card from Hambry's shirt but the mere thought of touching it made her feel ill.

"But what the hell for?" O'Doul asked.

"The last time I saw one of those business cards," Mackenzie said, "it was on the windshield of my car. On the back, someone had written 'Stop looking.' I guess this is just another warning."

"But the case is dead, right?" Penbrook said. "I mean, until this latest murder occurred and then the vagrants that your boy Peterson thinks are linked...why would it resurface again? We're talking what...twenty years of silence and then this shit?"

"It's a good question," Mackenzie said.

"God, this is awful," O'Doul said, making himself tear his eyes away from Hambry's body.

"I'll call it in," Penbrook said. He looked back at Mackenzie and Ellington. "How about you two? You need anything else here before it gets crowded?"

"No," Mackenzie said sharply. And then, without saying so much as another word, she turned her head and left the apartment.

***

Mackenzie was so overcome with emotion when she got back to the car that she was literally shaking. She was scared, she was pissed off, and she had never felt so defeated. And to make it even worse, she knew that on the other side of the country, there was a case waiting for her that still had no leads. Not a single fucking lead.

She did not cry often—and she decided that she would not do it there, either—but she felt the sting of tears of frustration wanting to be spilled. She gripped her hands into tight fists, her fingernails slightly digging into her flesh.

She heard footsteps behind her. Certain that it was Ellington coming to check on her, she did her best to push the turmoil of emotions away. She held her breath for a moment, squeezed her fists even tighter, and then pushed it all down.

And that's why you're going to end up spending a fortune in therapy when you retire, she thought to herself.

"Hey," Ellington said, stepping in close to her. He reached out for her hand but she did not give it.

She shook her head and found it hard to look at him. "This thing is wrecking me," she said. "Five minutes ago, before we went in there, I was excited. I was jumping out of my skin to get up there and end this whole thing—with my dad and his killer. With the business cards. But now...it's all different. This fucker is just playing with me."

"So you and I stay here," he said. "I think McGrath would allow it. We stay here and you and I will do what we can do to bring this thing to a close."

This time, he took her hand a little forcefully. He gave it a reassuring squeeze. And although she could tell he wanted to draw her close to him, he knew that she did not care for physical touch or intimacy when she was feeling distressed. It warmed her heart to see that he knew this about her and was respecting it.

"No," she said, shaking her head. "I have to close the priest case. I'm not going to leave it to another agent."

"He's got Yardley on it," Ellington said. "She's pretty sharp."

"I know. But...I have to. I have to and—"

"I know," he said.

And Mackenzie was pretty sure he *did* know. He knew that she could not half-ass something. She *had* to wrap up the case waiting for her back in DC.

What Ellington maybe *didn't* know, however, was that once it was wrapped up, she intended to put all of her time, focus, and energy on her father's case and nothing else.

After tonight, she had no choice.

Whoever was behind it had essentially forced her hand tonight. And she was going to see to it that the bastard paid.

But first, she had to know everything there was to know here in Nebraska. And that meant she had one more stop to make.

"Do you have Kirk Peterson's number?" she asked.

"I do," Ellington said. "But he's not really reliable."

This struck her as odd because from what she remembered of him, Peterson was a pretty sharp guy—dedicated to his job and a hound for the details.

"I need to talk with him before I head back home," she said.

Ellington seemed to weigh this out for a moment. In the end, he pulled the number up, called it for her, and handed over the phone. As it started to ring in her ear, she couldn't help but notice that Ellington looked troubled by something.

He's not happy I'm calling Peterson, she thought.

But before she had time to wonder why, Peterson answered the phone and it was too late to ask any questions.

CHAPTER TWENTY

When Ellington parked the car in the parking lot of the Waffle House Peterson had asked them to meet him at, the place was pretty quiet. It was nearing 10 o'clock and the place was pretty dead. Before they got out of the car, Ellington placed a hand on her shoulder, indicated that he wanted her to wait.

"There's something I should tell you before we go in there," he said.

"What's that?"

"I don't know how you remember this Peterson guy, but something has happened to him since that last time you saw him. The dude seemed a little off to me but I figured it was just some eccentric detective bullshit. But then I heard a few things from the agents who have worked with him. They say he's just gone sort of dark. Not in a loose cannon sort of way, but in an almost gothic sense. He's very dreary and quiet."

"That's not how I remember him."

Ellington shrugged. "I guess it's a good thing I said something, then. I only spoke to him twice since I've been here and he was helpful and all. He's just...I don't know. Something about him creeps me out."

"Okay. You've warned me. Let's get moving."

He said nothing else, though it was clear he wanted to. They got out of the car and went inside among the smell of sweet waffle batter and syrup. Peterson was sitting at a table by himself. He had the look of a man who hadn't slept in ages, as if he might be auditioning for the role of a vampire in a campy horror movie.

Oddly enough, his state made her think of her younger sister, Stephanie. In his dour state, he looked almost broodingly handsome—the sort of borderline goth type that Stephanie usually went crazy for.

Stephanie, she thought. *My God, I haven't given her a second thought in ages.*

He gave them both a little nod of recognition as they came to the table and sat down. "Good to see you again, Agent White."

"Same here," she answered as she and Ellington sat down. "I hate to seem bossy, but I'd like to get back to DC as soon as possible, so I don't really have a lot of time for formalities."

"Just as well," Peterson said. "This fucking case is driving me crazy and I'm just about done talking about it. Dealing with it. Whatever. The bureau is deep into it now, anyway. I feel like I can let it go."

"That's the thing," she said. "I know how the bureau works. That's why I wanted to talk to you. I know you have a different work ethic as the bureau. So I was hoping you could tell me about the possible links between the vagrant cases you've been working, my father, and these damned business cards."

"Yeah, I heard on the scanner there was another one at the Hambry residence," Peterson said. "Proof positive that this whole case is just way too over my head."

"How so?" she asked.

"Well, there's just no end to it. It reminds me of one of those conspiracy theories where the more you dig, the more questions you have. The rabbit hole just goes deeper and deeper."

"And how did this whole co-op thing start for the two of you?" Ellington asked.

"Almost a year ago, I came out here when Peterson was working a case about...hell, I barely remember now."

"Well, it was initially a domestic thing," Peterson recalled. "A wife wanted me to snoop on her husband—a guy named Jimmy Scotts. She thought he was cheating and spending their kid's college savings. What I found was that he was dealing with drug cartel nonsense out of New Mexico. But before I could make the call to break the news to his wife, he turned up dead. His wife found him dead in their bedroom from two bullet holes to the back of the head. She was in the house when it happened. No memory of hearing gunshots."

"Shit," Ellington said, looking at Mackenzie. "Like your dad."

"Yeah, but no known connection at all," Mackenzie said.

"I never found one, either."

"So how do the vagrants line up with the murders of my father and Jimmy Scotts?" Mackenzie asked.

"The point-blank shots to the top of the head. Same kind of gun is used every time. And those business cards...there was one on every single one of the bodies."

"How many are we talking?" Mackenzie asked.

"Three, so far. Two confirmed homeless during the time of their murders. The other one wasn't homeless, but extremely poor. He was just getting his life back together."

"Any connection between the three?"

"Nothing solid. Two of them attended the same soup kitchen. One of them worked together with the brother of another in the past to rob a woman at gunpoint for the sixty bucks she had in her pocketbook. But nothing else."

"Would you mind sending me all of your case files?"

Peterson chuckled. "I can. But there's not much to them. I didn't really take many notes."

"Forgive me for asking," she said, "but what happened? You seemed like a different person when you and I last met."

"I guess I was. But this fucking case...it got to me. I got obsessed. And it didn't help that the third one of these murdered vagrants was a twelve-year-old kid."

"Oh God," Mackenzie said.

"So please forgive me if I'm not all sunshine and rainbows."

"Easy," Ellington said sternly.

The two men stared at one another from across the table, sizing one another up. Peterson was the first to look away—not out of intimidation but because he seemed bored.

"Yes, I can send you what I have," Peterson said. "Are they really planning to send DC agents out here while the Omaha guys are running it?"

"No idea," Mackenzie said. "But you know this case is very close to me. Any help would be appreciated."

"Of course," Peterson said. "Now, I haven't eaten in about a day or so. So I intend to gorge myself on walnut pancakes and crepes. You guys are welcome to join me."

Mackenzie almost accepted. The fact that seeing him had for some weird reason made her think of Stephanie was still bothering her. And something about him seemed to scream for some sort of human interaction. Yet, at the same time, it was very clear that he was not a fan of human interaction anymore.

"Thanks, but I need to get on a plane as soon as possible," she answered. "But thanks again for meeting with me."

"Sure. I'll email you what I have as soon as I get back home."

Mackenzie nodded as she and Ellington got up from the table. They headed back to the parking lot, Mackenzie quiet and reflective.

"I told you," Ellington said. "Something got under his skin *bad*."

"You were right," she said.

A twelve-year-old kid, she thought. *The same people who killed my father are the kinds of people who have no issues killing children.*

It certainly gave the case a new perspective.

And as something churned within her heart, Mackenzie also realized that it gave her a whole new motivation to figure out just what in the hell was going on.

But first…there was a mess in DC waiting for her that she needed to clean up.

CHAPTER TWENTY ONE

They caught the red-eye flight back to DC. The plane held a thin crowd; fewer than thirty passengers filled the seats and the cabin was peacefully quiet. Mackenzie had allowed herself to drift off for a bit and when she woke up, her watch read 4:36 a.m. She thought she might have had another nightmare but if she had, she barely remembered it.

Good riddance, she thought as she sat up gingerly in her seat. She wasn't sure where they were, what cities lurked below in the darkness, and she really didn't care. In the air, over the country and all of her problems, she almost felt free.

It was the most peaceful she had felt since discovering the business card pinned to Hambry's bloody shirt. Of course, she couldn't stop thinking about the murdered vagrants, either. Especially the child. She wondered if Peterson had emailed her the documents yet.

For the second time since meeting him at the Waffle House, Mackenzie wondered how something could so harshly affect someone. When she had first met Peterson, he had been strikingly handsome, good-natured, and driven. But the obsession with his case and, apparently, the murder of those vagrants had pushed him somewhere else—somewhere dark. She'd heard about it before. She'd once read the profile of a retired cop who had ended up shooting a ten-year-old in the midst of a gunfight on a busy urban street. The cop had not only retired; he had gone on to battle severe depression, leaving his family and eventually killing himself in a motel room, placing a gun eerily similar to her service weapon into his mouth.

Mackenzie shook the thought away and tried to reorient herself. Ellington was reading a paperback someone had left behind from a previous flight. He never slept while flying—just another of the hundreds of tidbits she had learned about him during their time together. She loved getting to know him and even now, knowing that she'd have an exhausting day waiting for her when they landed, she looked forward to every day with him.

"Well, good morning, beautiful," he said with a smirk.

"Where are we?" she asked, still a little groggy.

"The last we heard from the captain, we should land in about half an hour. How are you doing? Your nap help?"

"I don't know yet."

He nodded and set the paperback down on his knee, a battered old Vince Flynn book.

"Look," he said. "I figure I'll go ahead and say this while you're still sort of sleepy so you can't get too upset. But after seeing you so shaken up tonight, I want to go along with you when you settle up and go after this Barker Antiques killer."

"But I don't think it's—"

"Aw, I'm sorry," he said, taking her hand. "You're mistaken. It wasn't a question. I'm just letting you know so we can save the argument later. You have no say. I know you think you're hot shit and all, but this is one instance where I'm going to put my foot down."

His tone and grin made her realize that it was all coming from a place of love. Even the *I know you think you're hot shit* comment.

"But this isn't—"

"This thing...this you and me thing," he said. "It goes beyond the bedroom. It goes beyond this feeling that I'll go ahead and admit is very likely love. I'm in this with you. I'm going with you."

"You think McGrath will even allow it?" she asked.

She had to admit...she liked the idea of Ellington being by her side when she would finally be able to put all of her attention on the Barker Antiques case. After talking with Peterson, she realized just how deep it went. It just made sense to go into it with a partner she trusted and knew she could rely on.

"If he doesn't, we can always threaten to quit," Ellington said.

"Oh, you sweet talker, you."

She leaned over and kissed him. It was amazing how natural it felt, how normal.

"So, how do you think Hambry is connected?" he asked. "Any theories?"

"A few. There were always unfounded rumors about my father being involved in some shady stuff. I've secretly wondered if one of the reasons Jimmy Scotts was murdered a few months back was because the man who killed my father is maybe part of some generational thing. Like, maybe a family tree that skewed a little too hard. Maybe he's raising his next generation to carry out whatever messed up work he was working on. It would explain the gap between my father's death and the murder of Jimmy Scotts, I guess. And then there's the vagrants..."

"What about them?" Ellington asked.

"Well, I don't know enough about the cases, but vagrants being killed in an almost execution style would either suggest some sort of weird gang activity that would likely be drug related. Or maybe someone is just trying to send a message."

"But what message? And to who?"

"I don't know. Maybe it's both things. Maybe if my father *was* involved in something he didn't want his family to know about, it was drug related. Or maybe even weapons related. There were cases from back then of delivery trucks getting caught at the border, stocked with heroin, weapons, you name it."

Ellington considered it and nodded his approval. "Yeah, it's a theory, I guess."

"And theories aren't strong enough," she said. "Which is why I'm shifting gears now. When we land, I'm one hundred percent on this priest case. I have to be. I have to have some sort of progress on *something* or I'm going to lose my mind."

They held hands and enjoyed the silent hum of the airplane as they neared DC. She was pretty sure she drifted off once more during their approach, wrapped up in the safety of having him beside her. One moment, she was looking at their interlocked hands and the next, she was jarred awake by the landing gear contacting the runway.

"All of these little naps," Ellington whispered into her ear, "and you're bound to have some dragon breath."

"I haven't had a shower in nearly two days and I've been traveling far too much during that time," she said. "The way my breath smells is the least of my concerns."

As they unbuckled and waited for permission to get off of the plane, Mackenzie checked her phone. Just like when she had landed in Nebraska, notifications kept popping up as her service resumed now that they were on the ground.

She went over her texts first and the first one was enough.

"Damn," she said.

"What is it?" Ellington asked. But the tone in his voice indicated that he already knew.

"Another body," she said. "Another priest."

CHAPTER TWENTY TWO

After a while, the feeling of exhaustion had become just a minor irritation to Mackenzie. She now felt a lack of sleep in the same way some people dealt with a bothersome headache that came and went from time to time. When she and Ellington pulled into the rear parking lot of St. Peter's Cathedral, it was 6:20 a.m. and Mackenzie had enjoyed about six total hours of sleep in the past thirty-six hours. She'd suffered through worse, but the jet lag made it even worse than normal.

The scene waiting for them behind the church was surreal. The first thing she noticed was a large black canopy that stretched from the wall of the church, stretching about three feet out into the parking lot. It stood about twelve feet tall, draped outward like some weird demonic Halloween decoration. A few cops were standing outside of the canopy, mixed in with a few other FBI agents.

Saw horses and traffic cones had been set up to block entrances into the back lot; Mackenzie and Ellington themselves had been ushered down the entering street by a policeman, as all streets leading to the back lot of the church had also been blocked off.

They walked directly to the canopy, where Yardley and Harrison were speaking rather animatedly to a police officer. Harrison saw them first, nudged Yardley, and pointed her toward them. After excusing herself from the officer, Yardley, with Harrison on her heels, met them at the front of the canopy.

"What's with the circus tent?" Ellington asked.

"This one's bad," Yardley said. Her voice was stern and a little deflated. "We have a crew coming in to take it down."

"Take it down?" Mackenzie asked.

"Just have a look for yourself," Yardley said. She stepped aside to give them clear access into the canopy.

The entrance was just two sides of the canopy falling down and overlapping. Ellington had been dead on with his description. It looked exactly like a circus tent, only one that had been erected by a morbid and particularly demented carnival barker. Upon closer inspection, Mackenzie saw that the canopy had been constructed by steel poles that were bolted into the back wall of the church. It had been a hurried job, indicating that what waited for them under the canopy was bad enough to want the bureau to hide it from the public at all costs.

They stepped under the canopy and it was like walking into some strange underground chamber. Only this one was lit by two small floodlights that had been placed on the floor. They were angled toward the church, illuminating the gruesome scene that rested against the wall.

A huge cross had been propped against the back wall. A priest had been nailed to it in the same way the other three had been displayed. This priest had been set up to look exactly like the figure of Jesus Christ, right down to the crown of thorns and the thin white sheet covering his privates that was seen in all depictions of the crucifixion.

At the foot of the cross, there was a shirt, a pair of pants, a wallet, a half-used roll of Lifesavers, and thirty-six cents in change.

Quietly, Yardley and Harrison entered the canopy. Yardley came up beside Mackenzie and spoke in a low voice.

"Father Wade Coyle," she said. "Fifty-one years of age. We've spoken to others within the church. He would have been here alone between the hours of five and eight, stationed at the confessional inside."

Mackenzie nodded, still taking it all in. The top of the cross nearly touched the top of the canopy. The slabs of wood were massive, and Coyle's feet were easily three feet off of the ground. For someone to have done this by themselves…it was almost impossible. They'd have to be determined and strong—and would have to have a very straightforward plan to follow.

She approached the cross and looked up at Coyle. The slit along the right side was much more noticeable this time. It actually looked as if it had intentionally been roughly cut. She looked to the hands, then the feet; the hands had been nailed and the feet bound, just like all of the others.

There are four now, she thought. *It should be easier to decipher what's important and what is not.*

She went through a mental checklist as she observed the body. She did her best to observe every inch—a next to impossible task being that his feet were roughly three feet off of the ground.

The types of nails used are leading us nowhere, she thought. *Forensics has come up with nothing there. Same goes for the bailing wire around the feet. They're all too common to figure out who might have bought some at a certain time. So that's basically ruled out in regards to finding a lead.*

It's going to come down to the planning. To put this cross together and nail someone to it without anyone seeing it...the killer had to plan it. He has to know the church and the area. But to know all of the churches that are involved, he's really canvassing this thing out.

So it's going to come down to how the killer knows the victims and the churches. This is going to come down to relationships and connections. His ability to plan and carry out these murders without anyone seeing him or leaving any evidence—he's far too careful. We could wait for him to slip up but by then...how many more would be killed?

She was barely aware of Harrison slowly coming up from behind. He looked down at the foot of the cross, at the scattered items there.

"You get the meaning of the things scattered at the bottom of the cross?" Harrison asked.

"Yeah," Mackenzie said as some of the stories she'd heard in Sunday school came back to her. "When Christ was crucified, the soldiers and onlookers cast lots at his feet for his belongings."

"So are we to think this guy saw Coyle as Christ?" Ellington asked.

"I think we have to consider it," Mackenzie asked.

Someone else came into the canopy, entering with a little less silence than Yardley and Harrison. Mackenzie turned and saw McGrath coming in with a strut in his step. He did not look mad or upset, but *very* concerned.

"Well," he said, "let's consider it as quickly as we can. There's a massive shit storm brewing on this. I'm receiving calls this morning that are making me uneasy. Whether we like it or not, this case is going to make national headlines. It also has the potential to be one of those cases that's going to bring the religious zealots out of the woodwork. And once they come out, the angry and bitter atheists are going to come out, too. It's going to get bad before it gets better, I can tell you that."

"What kind of calls?" Mackenzie asked.

"The Vice President, for one," he said. "He was here just yesterday to worship. *Yesterday.* And he chewed into me for the bureau not having caught this guy yet. And he also let me know that there are a lot of people on the Hill that are worried about this case."

"So in other words," Mackenzie said, "if we don't wrap it up soon, we'll also have a media and politics fiasco to contend with while working it?"

"That's the long and short of it," McGrath said. "But listen…I've come here personally to speak with Agents White and Ellington. Yardley and Harrison, could you please wait for me outside. I'll debrief you as best as I can in just a moment."

Harrison started walking for the exit right away, as dutiful as ever. Yardley was a little slower to move, though. Mackenzie understood her reaction; she felt like she was playing second fiddle, which was never a good feeling. She cast one final look back at the scene before making her exit back out into the parking lot.

McGrath stepped closer to Mackenzie and Ellington. She didn't think the man had ever stood so close to her before. It was a little intimidating.

"Look. I have some information that isn't classified, per se, but it would cause some bombs to go off at the White House and within Congress. And I think it might be information that could build a lead. I just got the info about an hour ago. In addition to the Vice President calling, I've also had calls from two congressmen and a senator. Through those calls, I learned something about Father Coyle here that isn't exactly public knowledge."

"Not more scandals of abuse and sexual misconduct, I hope," Mackenzie said.

"No, not this time," McGrath said. "I've heard the same story from two different sources now, and I trust both of them. Apparently, Wade Coyle had a serious beef with a man who nearly got on staff with St. Peter's as a deacon. The man was rejected at the last minute—literally two weeks before he would have been given title of deacon here. And the news came directly from Coyle. There was some social media bickering between the two, which Coyle wisely stopped engaging in. But there was then an altercation outside of Coyle's home a little less than three weeks ago. From what I gather, the altercation occurred about two weeks after the rejection. At least a dozen people in the neighborhood saw it."

"What's the connection to the people who called you?" Ellington asked.

McGrath shook his head. "I can't get into those details. The most I'll tell you is that there are certain scandals the Catholic Church has worked hard to keep dead. And sometimes they need some help with that."

"So do we have a name for this rejected deacon?" Mackenzie asked.

"Yes," McGrath said. "And I want the two of you—and *just* the two of you—to be as discreet as possible on this. Do whatever you need to do the moment you leave here. I want *only* the two of you speaking to this man and then as far as I'm concerned, I'm taking the leash off. Do whatever you can to wrap this case before it becomes even more of a nightmare."

"How much time do you think we have?"

McGrath shrugged. "I'd say two days. Maybe three, but that would be pushing it. You know how news travels around here— especially bad news." He sighed and whispered the next part. "The rejected deacon is a man by the name of Colton McDaniel. I'll send you his address in a few minutes. And seriously...after that text, you go quiet. Update me when needed, but you two become shadows. Got it?"

"Yes sir," Mackenzie said.

"How were things in Nebraska?" McGrath asked.

"Frustrating," Ellington said.

"There are more questions than anything else," Mackenzie said.

McGrath waved it away and shrugged. "I'll request a report from the Omaha field office. For now, you two get going. I'm counting on you. Don't let me down, okay?"

And with that, McGrath turned on his heel to leave.

"No pressure, right?" Ellington said, reaching out and giving her hand a squeeze.

"Right. No pressure."

They walked out from beneath the canopy. As they stepped back into the morning, the sun just starting to cast light on the back lot, a work truck was being allowed to come onto the scene. The small crane on the back of it showed its intent—this was the crew that would be taking Coyle and his cross down.

As she and Ellington marched quickly back to their car, Mackenzie caught sight of Yardley and Harrison. Yardley was watching them go, doing what she could not to appear jealous. They exchanged a little nod of acknowledgment as Mackenzie got in the passenger's seat.

"Ellington," she said. "I know we're in a hurry but I really need a shower. And coffee. Can we make those happen in the next hour?"

"Yeah," he said. "You do kind of stink."

And even that little jab failed to lift her spirits. She was too busy focusing on the comment McGrath had made to them.

I'm counting on you. Don't let me down...

He'd never expressed such desperation before and now that he had shown this bit of vulnerability, Mackenzie couldn't help but felt that she was going to do exactly that.

CHAPTER TWENTY THREE

They stopped by their apartment and were very professional about it. While Mackenzie took a shower and allowed herself a single minute to just soak and relax, Ellington put on coffee. Mackenzie toweled off, got dressed, and found a cup of coffee ready and waiting for her.

"Bless you," she said.

"Sure thing. So hey...I've been on Twitter, looking at this exchange between Coyle and McDaniel. It's interesting to say the least."

"Anything that would point to motive?"

"No. Just the rejection in and of itself. But I'm seeing hints from Coyle's account from what it might have all been about. Something about a past that would easily deter his duties as deacon. Of course, it's all veiled. He was trying to be professional without calling McDaniel out by name."

"Well, maybe McDaniel will open up about his past if he knows that Coyle has been killed."

"How do you know McDaniel isn't the killer?"

"Oh, I don't. He might very well be. But I'm not going to jump right into that assumption just based on some bitching on Twitter."

"Fair enough," he said, checking his watch. "If we leave now, we can probably get to his house before morning rush hour kicks in...almost certainly before he leaves for work."

She nodded and grabbed her coffee, already heading for the door. "What does he do anyway? Do we know?" "He owns a small landscaping company. He only does it part time, from what I can tell. He's writing a book on the side."

"What about?" she asked.

"New Age mysticism and its effects on Western religions."

"Maybe that's a glimpse into that checkered past Coyle was hinting at," Mackenzie suggested. And as the words came out of her mouth, something about them just felt right.

Maybe this is it, she thought. Perhaps it was simply being invigorated by the shower, but her mind was clearer, her hope for progressing on the case brighter. *Maybe this is the one lead we've been looking for.*

With coffee in hand and a restored motivation pushing her along, she stepped out the door behind Ellington and into a morning she hoped would finally yield some results.

***

They'd made pretty good time but just barely caught Colton McDaniel before he left for work. He lived in a respectable subdivision twenty minutes from Capitol Hill. It was a quaint house with a nicely maintained yard, the result of his profession. When Ellington parked the car in front of his house, McDaniel was loading a weed eater into the back of a small work truck with a decal along the side that read McDaniel Landscaping.

Colton McDaniel looked to be about forty-five or so. He was slightly overweight and had the slightly chubby cheeks that, a decade or so earlier, might have made him look younger than his age. Now, though, they seemed to hint at more weight to come as he got older.

The moment McDaniel saw them get out of the car, he let out a curse. He then slammed the tailgate of the truck and rolled his eyes.

"FBI?" he said.

"Yes," Ellington said. "Agents Ellington and White. You look annoyed, sir. And not very surprised to see us."

McDaniel shrugged. "I got a call twenty minutes ago. I know about Wade. Then about five minutes ago, I got another call. From a news program, asking if I had anything to say."

Man, they're moving fast, Mackenzie thought.

"And do you know about the three other religious leaders that have been in the news over the last week and a half or so?" Mackenzie asked.

"I do. No one will come out and admit it, but there's an undercurrent of absolute fear running through the religious community of this city right now. So yes…I know."

"I suppose it goes without saying that we'd like to ask you a few questions," Mackenzie said.

"I figured as much. Although I don't know how I could help you. Unless you're here to see if our little altercation in front of his house got me so angry that I decided to murder him. If that's why you're here, I *can* help you. I didn't do it."

"Tell us about that altercation in front of his house," Mackenzie said.

"It was stupid on my part. But…I worked *hard* to get to where I was. I devoted my time and my heart to God. I was excited. I felt

106

like I was finally achieving my life's purpose—to work toward the wrong I had done in the past. And then Coyle and whoever else makes the decisions for St. Peter's got scared and closed the door in my face. It's more than rejection. It's borderline demoralizing. So I went to his house to give him a piece of my mind. We ended up in the front yard because he wouldn't invite me in. And it got heated."

"What did you do in your past that was so bad that you decided to devote your life to the church?" Mackenzie asked.

"I was big into New Age teachings," he said. "For a while, I even dabbled in Wicca. I was a lost young man, looking for answers in any place other than the Catholicism my parents shackled me to through my childhood."

"And that bothered Coyle?"

"No. Not at first. I've been working on a book about it. About how the influx of New Age nonsense is more harmful to Christianity than we think. I've been shopping the pitch around and finally got an agent. That agent got me a book deal pretty quickly and I think *that's* what freaked Wade out. To think that a man within his church would be associated with a book filled with some controversial topics, even if it *was* all to promote the glory of God. It scared him and they cut me loose."

"Do you intend to seek a position as a deacon elsewhere?" Mackenzie asked. She felt a little foolish, not quite knowing how the process worked.

"I don't know," McDaniel said. "If I've got reporters already calling me about his death, I don't see my name being held in a good light anymore. This has the potential to ruin me."

He's far too worried about the call from the reporters, she thought. *He's more worried about the reporters and media than the fact that the FBI showed up at his house.*

She was pretty sure things would check out, but she asked anyway: "Mr. McDaniel, where were you last night?"

"Until about midnight, I was in the garage fixing this weed eater," he said, hitching a thumb to the back of the truck. "After that, I went to bed. My son can vouch for that because he was being sneaky trying to play his Xbox after midnight. I yelled at him a little about it."

"And is he inside?"

"No. He caught the bus for school about ten minutes before you got here."

Not that it matters, Mackenzie thought. *He's not the guy.*

"Thank you for your t—" she started, but was interrupted by the ringing of her cell phone.

She saw Harrison's name and number pop up, so she excused herself by turning away and taking a step toward the car.

"Hey, Harrison, what is it?"

"Wherever you and Ellington are, turn around and come to the Third District police station."

"Why? What's happened?"

"Some in this case might say *a miracle*," Harrison joked. "We've got our guy. We've got the killer."

CHAPTER TWENTY FOUR

There were two police officers waiting for them when they arrived and Mackenzie could tell right away that they were just as confused as she was. They did, however, look slightly relieved when she and Ellington got out of the car.

"What the hell is going on?" Mackenzie asked the officer who was flanking them on the left.

"Some guy just came in this morning and confessed to it all."

"Is there any evidence against him?"

"He knows more than he should about the crime scenes," the officer said. "Honestly, I don't know that much. There's only a few officers and a detective on this. Two of your agents showed up about twenty minutes ago."

The officers escorted them into the Third District headquarters and then moved quickly. They walked through a small bullpen-type area and then down a hall. At the end of the hall, several people were milling around. Two of them were in telltale bureau suits: Harrison and Yardley.

The two escort officers gave them both a little wave and then hurried back down the hallway toward the bullpen. They were apparently very anxious to get as far away from this scene as possible. Mackenzie and Ellington proceeded toward the small group of people at the end of the hallway. Beyond them, there was a left turn.

The interrogation rooms, Mackenzie assumed.

"What do we know about him?" Mackenzie asked Yardley as they joined the other two agents.

"I'm still catching up. We're getting updates as quickly as the bureau can send them. The officers here are trying their best to help with public records. But as of right now, we know this: At seven forty-five this morning, Joseph Simmons came in through the front doors here and started screaming that he needed to be punished. He couldn't take it anymore. Someone tried to come over and calm him—a woman who had just come on duty—and he punched her in the jaw. He's been in custody for about hour now and he seems to know an awful lot about these priest cases. And I hate to say it, but he just...I don't know. He *feels* crazy."

109

"Have you spoken with him yourself?" Mackenzie asked.

"For about three minutes. But then my phone started blowing up with information from the bureau about him so I stepped out. By the way, everything I received, I forwarded to your email."

"Thanks," Mackenzie said. She stepped slightly away from the gathered crowds and their murmurs of conversation. She pulled up her email and found the two emails that had come from Yardley in the last half an hour and read over them. Bit by bit, it seemed like things were starting to fall into place. The way they had gotten their killer might have been anticlimactic but at least they seemed to have him now…one way or the other.

She read through the PDFs the bureau had sent and quickly got a clear picture of Joseph Simmons. An admitted runaway at the age of fifteen, he had lived on the streets of Richmond, Virginia, until the age of twenty-one. Working a few manual labor jobs at farms and construction sites for a few years, he managed to make enough money to support himself, eventually landing a steady job at a Target in Richmond. By the age of twenty-eight, he moved to DC, where he became a systems safety trainee and then assistant manager at a packing warehouse. It was a great story of lifting yourself up by the bootstraps…if not for where Simmons seemed to go a bit off the rails three years ago.

He had been arrested three years ago outside of a bar for beating up a woman. He had then hit the boyfriend with a brick, nearly hospitalizing him. He did a brief stint in prison for the assault and when he was released, he was arrested for a string of assault-and-run cases in the DC area. He was eventually released when the actual suspect was found. But in the two years that had passed since then, Simmons had come forward to confess to two other crimes. One was for the theft of a car and the beating of a prostitute *after* her services had been rendered.

For that, he *had* been found guilty.

But when he came forward to confess to the murder of a juror during a high-profile courtroom drama last year, he was clearly innocent. He was released and sent to a psychiatrist.

And now here he was again. It was weird and it made no sense. In other words, it seemed to fit perfectly with this case.

"What do you think?" Harrison asked.

"I think it's at least worth a shot. His relentless habit of confessing to crimes is an attention-seeking behavior—especially for a very serious one he didn't commit. And if he's that desperate for attention, there's no telling what he's capable of."

Aside from her, Ellington, Yardley, and Harrison, there were two cops and a plainclothes detective in the hallway, all discussing what had happened this morning. One of the cops was laughing softly, but the detective looked grave.

"Who's in charge here?" she asked.

"You guys," the cop who had not been laughing said. "And good riddance, as far as I'm concerned. Just let us know if you need anything."

Mackenzie nodded and headed down the branched off hallway to the left. There were three rooms along this hall, the last of which was an interrogation room; the one beside it was the observation room, where she assumed the cops, the detective, and her fellow agents would be watching her.

She stepped into the interrogation room and found Joseph Simmons staring at her. His posture froze her for a moment. For a split second, she saw Gabriel Hambry, sitting there with a hole in his head and a business card pinned to his shirt.

She shook the thought away, taking in Simmons's gaze. He did not look nervous or out of sorts. He looked almost expectant, like a child who was sitting down for his birthday cake, knowing that the moment to blow out the candles was quickly approaching.

He wants attention, she thought. *And if he's the killer, he'll likely clam up and become difficult if he doesn't get it. I need to act like I'm impressed—and maybe even defeated that he came to us rather than us catching him.*

"So tell me," she said, feigning embarrassment. "Why now? Why are you coming to us now?"

"Because my work is done," Simmons said.

"Four victims," she said, making sure to keep her voice at a defeated volume and tone. "Why four?"

"I don't know. It's what I was told."

"Told by whom?"

Simmons tilted his head from one side to the other and bit at his bottom lip. Eventually, he shrugged and answered: "Because it's what they said. The voices."

"And what else do the voices tell you?" Mackenzie asked.

"Oh, I can't tell you that. They'd get very upset. Besides, I had to turn myself in. Let's face it…you were never going to catch me."

"Oh, we would have eventually," she said, doing her best to seem overly frustrated. She knew she wasn't much of an actress, but she also knew that Simmons wouldn't notice…so long as she fed his ego.

"Sure you would have," he said. He then let out a raspy laugh that sounded almost as rehearsed as Mackenzie's defeat.

"I have to know," Mackenzie said, sitting down across the small table from him. "With Coyle, how did you get that cross up? It must have weighed a ton."

"Well, the beams came from the church basement. They were props that were sometimes used for children's ministry. One of them even had a bolt halfway up from where it was used for some temporary construction project or something. I slid the boards right out the basement entrance. I propped one up against the back wall while I nailed Coyle's hands to the other one. Wrestling him up there was a feat, but I managed to get it done."

"By yourself?"

"Yeah," he said, as cocky as ever.

"What did you have against these men?" Mackenzie asked.

"The same thing everyone else in the world has against them. Their blind faith. Their ignorance and their willingness to lead others astray toward their invisible gods. Their hatred of homosexuals. Their greediness. Their sins that they try to cover up like a cat covering up shit in a litter box."

"But four was enough?" Mackenzie asked. She was pretty sure that if she tried circling back around, Simmons would get frustrated and be easier to trip up. Also, if he *was* the killer, the scattered conversation rather than a focus on his work would irritate him. "Is there some special relevance to the number four?"

"No," he said. "I just felt that my job was done. I told you. The voices said *four*. So I stopped at four."

She nodded but thought she had exposed the first flaw in him. To the basic questions where he could gloat, he had gone into detail. But when she asked him why he had stopped, his answer had been vague. Basic, even. Voices—a lame and clichéd answer.

"Well, you've done the right thing today, Mr. Simmons," she said. "Of course, I'm sure you know your rights, so do I really need to read them to you?"

A flicker of hesitation passed across his face. It was so quick that Mackenzie barely noticed it. "Yeah, I do."

"I figured," she said. "I mean, the thing with the stolen car and the prostitute several years back. And there was that other one, right? That other murder you confessed to…"

"That stupid bitch on the jury, you mean?"

"Yeah," Mackenzie said. "But you managed to slither away from that, didn't you?"

And then there it was again…a crack in his façade. She wasn't quite sure what it meant just yet but she knew for certain that he was hiding something.

"No, I didn't *slither away*," he said. "The idiot cops charged someone else with it. They let me go. And look what it got them. Four dead priests."

"So was this some sort of point you felt you needed to make? An incompetent system of law let you off so you had to show them how big of a mistake they made?"

"No. This was not a point. But maybe these four dead priests will—"

"Well, they weren't *all* priests," Mackenzie pointed out.

Simmons shifted uncomfortably as Mackenzie sat forward. Something was not right here. She could all but *see* it in the room. It was written all over his face and lingering in almost everything he said. Yes…something was not right here and she intended to turn the tables on him.

She gave him a moment to respond and when he didn't, she went on with her trickery.

"Yes, Coyle was a priest. So was Father Costas. But Woodall and Tuttle were not. Woodall was a pastor and Tuttle was a reverend. Not priests. Big difference there. Did you know that?"

"It doesn't matter," Simmons said. "They're dead now. Their lying voices are permanently shut."

"That's true," Mackenzie said. "Just one more question. You had set things out at the foot of Coyle's cross, but not at the others'. Why?"

"Just to have some extra fun. It's what they did with Jesus, you know? They even cast lots for his clothes."
"Yes, I know. But why the strange things you left at the foot of Coyle's cross? What was the significance? His wallet, his clothes, and the jelly beans."

Again, the slightest flicker of doubt showed on his face. But he covered it with a smile.

She didn't want to let the moment escape, so she pounced on it.

"Jelly beans," she said, as if the words were disgusting. "It's like you were making fun of him. Were they actually in his pockets?"

"Yeah," Simmons said. "Hell, I even had a few after I set the fucker up."

She then almost playfully ran her fingers along the surface of the table and got to her feet. "Someone will be in shortly to take your statement," she said.

"What are you—"

But Mackenzie was already out the door and headed back to where Yardley, Harrison, and Ellington were waiting.

"That was quick," Ellington said.

"He did it, didn't he?" Harrison asked.

"I'm not sure yet," she said. Although, honestly, she was leaning toward *no, absolutely not.* "Harrison, can you make a few calls? See if St. Peter's has any record of Joseph Simmons being among their congregation."

She then stepped over to the detective in charge. He looked uncertain as she sized him up but managed to meet her with a smile.

"Could I get you and the police to check on something for me?" she asked.

"Sure."

"I need a test done on his hands. He claims to have lugged those boards out of the basement of St. Peter's. But his hands show no sign of recent labor. Those boards were huge. There would be *some* sign, right?"

"Possibly," the detective said. "But if he was wearing gloves—"

"Then less than four hours have passed since he removed them. Wouldn't there be some trace evidence that he had worn gloves?"

"Possibly. But for tests like that, it might take a day or so to get results."

"That's fine. Can you see to it that it gets done?"

"Absolutely," the detective said, instantly reaching for his phone.

Ellington stepped away from everyone else and waved her over. She joined him and tried her best not to be sidetracked by the sly smile she gave him—a smile that, if they were alone, would have been rewarded with a lingering kiss.

"You don't think it's him, do you?"

"No, he couldn't answer basic questions about motive and interior details. I even purposefully got him to stumble over the facts and structure of the scene. I don't know exactly what details he knows about the crime scenes yet, though."

"Want me to get some of those details out of him?"

"Yeah, that would be a huge help."

"What are you going to do in the meantime?" he asked.

"I'm going to print out these files on his past confessions. He's seeking attention by confessing to these terrible crimes. And in the case of the prostitute and grand theft auto, he may have actually *committed* the crime. But murder…that's something different. I'm going to see if I can find a smoking gun."

"A smoking gun…to prove his *innocence*?"

She grinned at him as she turned to find a vacant office. "I guess we'll have to see."

***

While there had been ample excitement in the Third District station, Mackenzie and Ellington returned to FBI headquarters just before nine in the morning. Ellington had grilled Simmons on his knowledge of the crime scenes and Mackenzie had enjoyed plenty of time to dig through his files and align them with information that both the detective and Harrison had managed to get for her.

She had all of the information in front of her now as she sat across from McGrath at the small oak table in the back of his office. Ellington sat by her side, fully ready to support the gathered information and her theories.

"So what are your takeaways on Simmons?" McGrath asked.

"I think it's very convenient," Mackenzie said. "I had a gut feeling in the interrogation room that he wasn't our guy. And with information we've gathered this morning—some that just came to us within the last five minutes or so—I can tell you that I don't think Joseph Simmons is our guy."

"You just can't take a win the easy way, can you, White?" McGrath said.

"Follow me here, sir. We'll start with his history. He was a runaway. And even if things at home are terrible, psychiatrists believe that runaways, at their core, are crying out for love and attention. Before today, Simmons has confessed to two horrendous crimes. One of those crimes, the murder of a juror in a case from eight years ago, he was *clearly* innocent of. So why try to turn himself in for something like that?

"The prostitute beating checks out. It was him. But the details of the case also indicate that he was timid. He beat her badly but in a way that ensured he would not kill her. And now here he is again, confessing to a string of murders that is starting to get air time on the television. So I'm calling his bluff. If he wants jail time for some reason, he can get it for interfering in this case, but it sure as hell won't be for murder."

"What about the intimate details he knew about the crime scenes?" McGrath asked.

"I can answer that," Ellington said. "Agent Harrison got confirmation that up until about six months ago, Simmons attended St. Peter's church. He wasn't a regular by any means and he never actually joined the church, but people had seen him around enough to learn his name and be friendly with him. He even helped with a children's Bible school two summers ago. That's how he knew about the beams in the basement, right down to the bolts and grooves in the center of them.

"And honestly, the only other scene he knew anything about was the one at Living Word. And as of about two o'clock this morning, an article on CNN.com was reporting some pretty detailed descriptions of the scene that haven't made it to other news outlets yet. So if he was up on his studying of the cases, that's the ticket right there. There was nothing he knew about the Living Word scene that was not in this fresh CNN article."

"And then there's one last thing," Mackenzie said. "When I was talking to him, I intentionally tried to trip him up by throwing in fake information. I asked Simmons why he had set the stuff at the foot of Coyle's cross. I listed those items as *his wallet, his clothes, and the jelly beans.* Because the jelly beans was such an off-the-wall item that no one is going to think to even make up, Simmons jumped on it. Made jokes about jelly beans and how he'd even had one when he put the stuff at the foot of the cross."

"And it was Lifesavers, wasn't it?" McGrath asked.

"Yes, sir."

"Shit."

McGrath sat back in his chair, looking at the collected documents on the table in front of Mackenzie and Ellington.

"Here's what's going to happen," McGrath said. "We're going to hold Simmons for as long as we can. It'll shut the media up and it will calm down some of these nervous politicians and religious leaders. We won't give a name. But I can't hold that up for too long. So that means I need an *actual* suspect. So tell me…what next?"

Mackenzie knew what was next but she was reluctant to say anything because she hadn't even discussed it with Ellington yet.

"With your permission sir, I'm heading to Alexandria this evening."

"I told you," McGrath said. "Don't bother with my permission. Just get out there and find this fucking guy. What *is* out in Alexandria, though?"

"A recovery group for people who have been victims of sexual abuse. From what I've been told by Father Ronald Mitchell, the vast majority of the group meeting tonight has been involved in some sort of abuse at the hands of church leaders. I'm thinking I might be able to find some kind of thread through their stories and history."

"Then get going," he said. "But I'd prefer that Ellington stay here and help Yardley and Harrison."

"One more thing," Mackenzie said. "I need a list of people that the bureau has relied on in the past for information pertaining to religion or Biblical studies."

"I'll have it emailed to you within half an hour," McGrath said. "Anything else?"

Mackenzie wasn't quite sure how to handle the fact that McGrath was offering her pretty much anything. She felt that whatever she needed in that moment, he'd make sure to get it for her.

There was one thing on her tongue, one thing that begged to leap off and be spoken but she bit it back. Still, the thought echoed like thunder in her head.

When this case is done, I want full unhindered access to my father's case.

With that wish unspoken, she said: "No, sir."

With one final glance at Ellington, Mackenzie exited the office with the overwhelming sense that she was running a race that she was simply not going to win.

CHAPTER TWENTY FIVE

She didn't make it to the meeting in Alexandria before it started, so she had to enter as quietly as she could. The gathering was held in a small community center in the downtown area, the kind of place that smelled like stale coffee and dust. She found the room at the end of a long hallway and when she opened the door as quietly as she could and entered the room, only a few of the people noticed her. She got a few nasty looks as she found a lone metal folding chair in the back of the room and took a seat.

There was a woman sitting at the head of a semicircle of chairs—a woman named Barbara Francis. Mackenzie had called her and spoken with her on the way to Alexandria. Barbara headed up these meetings and although she had no history of abuse at the hands of the church herself, she did have a career in social work and psychiatry in the field of sexual abuse to make her a viable candidate to lead the group.

Because no one made a fuss or asked questions when she entered the room, Mackenzie assumed that Barbara had already told those in attendance that she would be stopping by to pay a visit. Mackenzie could not begin to imagine what the lives of these people must be like, having lived through such a trauma. She did her best to remain quiet and attentive, listening to each person who took the time to share.

What struck her the most was that there seemed to be no real age limit to the victims. There was a girl with her mother, the girl having been abused sometime last year at the age of thirteen. There was an older man who had just celebrated his sixtieth birthday who had been molested and abused between the ages of nine and twenty-five, told by his priest that if he told his family and caused any trauma to his mother and father, surely God would make sure he went to Hell when he died.

Mackenzie was spared the gory details of any single story but got to see glimpses of the pain and torment that some of these people went through. There were fourteen of them in all and no one effect seemed to be the same. For some it was a daily fear of physical contact from anyone, even loved ones. For others it was periodic nightmares that would stick with them for days. But through it all there was the sense of injustice—of how the men who had abused them had seen some form of punishment but nothing even close to matching the severity of their crimes.

She couldn't help but feel a bit like a voyeur as she sat in the back of the room. She almost felt bad for being there and started to wonder if coming here had been a mistake.

The meeting broke up an hour later. When everyone got up from their seats, Barbara nodded back toward Mackenzie.

"I'm sure some of you noticed our visitor," Barbara said. "And I appreciate you allowing her to sit in with us today. This is Agent Mackenzie White, with the FBI. She's currently working a case that deals with some of the pain that most of you have all been through. She has a few questions, so if you'd be willing to help, it would be appreciated."

Again, Mackenzie got irate glances. It was clear that no one in this room trusted her.

"I'll keep it short and sweet," she said. "Has anyone here ever had any sort of friendship or acquaintance with Father Henry Costas of Blessed Heart Catholic Church in Washington, DC?"

She got a few blank stares and shakes of the head. Two people had decided that they weren't sticking around for this line of questioning and walked right by her, straight out the door. She asked a few more questions, hoping to get some kind of lead. But assuming those in attendance were being truthful, no one at this meeting had ever met with any of the victims, nor had they ever heard of any of their friends or loved ones being abused or harassed by the victims in any way.

When it was clear that this meeting had essentially been a dead end, Mackenzie went quiet again, waiting for a moment to speak with Barbara Francis.

A few of those in attendance took a moment to speak with Barbara afterward. Others left right away, as if they couldn't wait to get out of the room and the forced reminder of what had happened to them. A few of them looked at Mackenzie, clearly not happy that she had been sitting in.

Mackenzie continued to hang back, wanting to speak with Barbara Francis. She had gotten a much better understanding of what those who suffered at the hands of religious leaders went through, but she had yet to find anything new that might help her to uncover the identity of a killer. She figured a woman with Barbara's background and education might help her to find some of those missing pieces.

As it turned out, it was Barbara who came to her when the room was mostly cleared. And she did not come alone. There was a woman of about thirty-five or so by her side. She was a naturally pretty woman but she wore her hair down over her face and she walked like someone who was expecting to fall in a hole at any moment. She also stayed very close to Barbara Francis as they came to where Mackenzie was still sitting against the back wall.

"Agent White," Barbara said. "First of all, thank you for not being a distraction during the meeting."

"Of course," Mackenzie said. "Thank you for allowing me to sit in and to ask my questions. I know it's a topic that the people who gather here hold as a very private matter."

"They do," Barbara said. "But, without giving them any details about your case, I was able to communicate to them that you were here to help—that you were working towards helping others. With all of that said, I think some are still very closed off and defensive when it comes to sharing their stories around people they don't know. All of that aside, though...I'd like you to meet Lindsay."

The bashful-looking woman nodded to her. She only glanced at Mackenzie for a moment, through, before her eyes returned to Barbara.

"Lindsay has given me permission to tell you why she is here. She isn't quite able to do it herself just yet. Lindsay, are you sure you wouldn't like to try to get it out?"

"I'm sure," Lindsay said quietly. "But you can go ahead."

"Lindsay's son was abused by a preacher that their family had been going to all of their life," Barbara said. "As far back as Lindsay's mother and father, her family has always attended this church and saw the preacher as a man that they loved and trusted. A man that would never hurt them or anyone else, for that matter.

"So you can imagine her surprise when her thirteen-year-old son came to her with a confession: that their seventy-two-year-old preacher engaged in some very explicit and pornographic acts with him. It was a demoralizing and—"

"That's too light," Lindsay said, apparently deciding that Barbara was being too lenient. "The bastard made my son...he made my son perform oral sex on him. And he *filmed* it."

Lindsay sounded like she might gag on the words as they came out. Barbara nodded, placing an arm around Lindsay. Mackenzie could tell that Lindsay wanted to cry but seemed almost unable to do so.

"So when her son came to her with this story," Barbara went on, "Lindsay and her husband scolded him, assuming he was making it up. When he became insistent and refused to go to church, they grounded him. After that, their son became distant and started acting out. He would start fights with his friends. He even took a swing at his father. And then, six months ago, her son committed suicide. It wasn't until then that Lindsay and her husband took their son's story seriously. They went to the police and after a brief investigation, they discovered more than twenty video clips saved to a portable hard drive. The preacher had done similar things with at least eight other children. There were also Polaroids in his closet, taken of pre-teens and children from as far back as the early eighties."

Mackenzie felt sick. And she could tell by the look on Barbara's face that the story wasn't over.

"The suicide was too much for the family," Barbara went on. "Lindsay's husband left her shortly afterwards. The preacher is in prison and a lot of the congregation blames Lindsay and her family."

"Why?" she asked.

"Because he was beloved," Lindsay spat. "The evidence is there, and they see it but they refuse to believe it. He even sent a note of apology to the church, which one of the deacons read out loud during a service."

"Agent White," Barbara said, "would you excuse me for a moment?"

"Sure."

Barbara slowly led Lindsay away, out of the room and into the hallway Mackenzie had come down about an hour ago. Mackenzie walked to the center of the room, needing to pace, needing to expel some of her nervous energy. She wasn't sure she had ever felt so sickened by a case before. Lindsay's story had made it significantly worse and it made Mackenzie feel almost helpless.

All of these stories of abuse only lead me deeper into the corruption and hidden sin within church organizations, she thought. *In the end, there's not even any guarantee that it's going to help me find the killer.*

She sat down in one of the chairs, feeling tired and weak.

And angry.

A few moments later, Barbara came back into the room. She was alone this time as she sat down beside Mackenzie.

"Did you find anything you were looking for?" Barbara asked.

"I don't know yet."

"Well, during the entire meeting, I had this thought in the back of my mind," Barbara said. "After I spoke with you about sitting in with us today, Lindsay's story came to mind and it stayed there pretty firmly. And it wasn't just because of the severity of the story, though it *is* a tragic one."

"Yeah, I'll say."

"I walked Lindsay out because the last part of the story is, for some reason, the hardest for her to hear. But I think you need to hear it. If you're looking for someone who is killing religious leaders of all denominations, I think it might tie in."

"How's that?" Mackenzie asked.

"Lindsay mentioned a letter that the preacher wrote. One of the deacons read it to the congregation the Sunday after the preacher went to prison. It was a short letter, but there was a comment in it that never really sat well with me. It seemed...I don't know. Odd, I guess."

"How did you hear it?" Mackenzie asked.

"Oh, I didn't. But someone in the church recorded it on their cell phone. I was sent a copy once I started to have weekly meetings with Lindsay. The letter talks all about sins of the flesh and repentance and sins. But near the end, he makes the comment about how he was glorifying the wrong things. Verbatim, he said, *I lost my love for Jesus at some point and started seeking something else. These poor children became my Jesus and I glorified them. And, as the Bible warns, when we place anything above our Lord, the repercussion is sin.*"

"So...he was what?" Mackenzie asked. "Sexually abusing them because he hated them? Because they were taking the place of God for him?"

"Perhaps," Barbara said. "There's so much to uncover there. The man is clearly mentally unstable. But yes...as far as I'm concerned, he was projecting abuse on these kids as a form of some sort of skewed worship. I've seen bits and pieces of the news stories about the case you're working on and that letter from the preacher came to me a few times. Especially the bit I just quoted you."

Mackenzie still felt ill beyond all comprehension but the theory did make a certain kind of sense.

"Let me ask you," Mackenzie said. "Do the people you work with ever manage to overcome the abuse?"

"Some do," she said. "It depends on the character of those abused and, of course, the extent of the abuse. I take it you've never dealt with a case in this arena?"

"Not to this extent, no."

Barbara nodded solemnly. "A word of warning," she said. "Don't let it get to you. Before you know it, you can become wrapped up in it. The stories are heartbreaking. And the fact that you can't fix them…it tears you up."

Mackenzie thought she was already getting a taste of that but said nothing. Certainly her few days of hearing a few stories was nothing in comparison to what Barbara had seen and heard.

"Thank you again for your willingness to let me attend," Mackenzie said.

"Of course," Barbara said. "I just hoped it helped."

She thought of the line from the preacher's letter that Barbara had just quoted and began to pick it apart.

These poor children became my Jesus and I glorified them. And, as the Bible warns, when we place anything above our Lord, the repercussion is sin.

"You know," she said. "I think it helped more than I thought it would."

He's not a victim, she thought. *What if he's not targeting these leaders out of revenge or hatred? What if he* loves *them? What if he's glorifying them through these mock crucifixions? What if he thinks they deserve the same death as Christ as a way to praise and worship them?*

"Thank you so much for your time," Mackenzie said.

She then turned on her heel and headed out the door. On the way to her car, she pulled up an email Harrison had sent her earlier in the day, just before she'd left Washington. The email was brief and to the point: just a name and phone number.

The contact information for the Biblical expert she had requested.

She placed the call before she was even back behind the wheel of her car as a sense of urgency started to flood her heart, replacing the dark sickness she'd felt just moments ago.

CHAPTER TWENTY SIX

She was back in DC just after eight o'clock. She got off of the expressway and bypassed FBI headquarters and her apartment altogether. Instead, she headed toward Park View, where she had set up her next meeting immediately upon leaving Barbara Francis in Alexandria. She allowed herself enough time to grab a quick drive-thru meal before heading to a small church she'd never heard of before.

She parked in front of Park View Church of Christ and headed straight for the ancient-looking front doors. Park View Church of Christ did not have the glitz and glamour of a Blessed Heart or Living Word, or even St. Peter's. It was a simple one-story church that was about the size of a modest house. It looked to have been built in the forties or fifties, complete with a steeple and actual bell in the top.

She found the front door unlocked, as she'd been told it would be. She walked through a small foyer and into a quaint sanctuary. Roughly fifty pews lined the floor and ornate but tasteful stained glass windows were situated along the walls. At best guess, Mackenzie assumed that the place could hold no more than three hundred people on any given Sunday.

At the front of the room, an older gentleman was painstakingly wiping down the top of an old grand piano. He looked up as she came down the center aisle that ran between the pews and gave her a small wave. He set his cloth down on the piano bench and met her halfway down the aisle.

"Agent White?" the man asked.

"Yes. And you're Benjamin Holland?"

"I am! It's good to meet you."

They shook hands and Mackenzie found that she liked Benjamin right away. She knew very little about him—only that the bureau had relied on him twice in the last ten years when they had needed someone to decipher clues that they had believed to be Biblical in nature. Benjamin Holland had come through in both instances, giving them enough information to bring a suspect in on one of the cases, and proving that there was nothing Biblical at all about certain clues in the other instance.

"So tell me how I can help," Benjamin said. "I've been following the story on the news and have been quite heartbroken. I knew all of those men; Reverend Tuttle and I had a habit of grabbing breakfast together nearly every Thursday morning for the better part of three years not so long ago."

"Well, for starters, I was wondering what you might be able to tell me about any instances of murder in the Bible that was done for the purpose of glorification."

Benjamin thought for a moment before he started walking to the front of the sanctuary. "Come with me for a moment, if you don't mind," he said. "I'll show you why I asked you to meet me here."

Finding this an odd answer to her question, Mackenzie followed along anyway. He led her through a door in the front of the sanctuary that led to a small room behind it. A few folding chairs propped against the wall indicated that it was a gathering place of some kind—maybe a place for potluck dinners or prayer meetings.

Another door awaited beyond this room. Benjamin opened it up and stepped inside, flipping on a light switch as he entered. Mackenzie found herself walking into a room where every wall was a bookcase. And every case seemed to be completely full. In the center of the room, there was a single couch and an old scarred coffee table. A Bible sat on the coffee table, opened up to a passage in Luke.

"This is my favorite room in all of Washington," Benjamin said proudly. "It's not mine, but I and three or four other leaders call it our own. Just about any answer I could ever need about life—spiritual and not—can be found in here. Have a seat, please."

Mackenzie sat down on the couch, looking around. She couldn't even venture a guess as to how many books were in this room. She saw Bibles in different translations and versions. She saw huge devotionals, memoirs and guidebooks, and so much more.

"Now," Benjamin said, standing by a shelf to his left. "In regards to your question about murder as a means of glorifying God. It can be answered a few different ways. It really all depends on who is asking. See, if you're asking from the perspective of someone who is deeply rooted in the law-driven religion of the Old Testament, I can give you lots of examples. But if you're more interested in the teachings and example of Christ, then it becomes much harder to answer."

"But it's the same book, right?" Mackenzie asked. She did not like feeling uneducated, but her lack of knowledge in Biblical teaching was shining through in that moment.

"It is," Benjamin said. "But you see, if you're leaning more toward Christ, then you must understand that his crucifixion was the answer to all of those burnt offerings and dead livestock on the alter rituals of the Old Testament. The Old Testament is rife with murder, some of it even ordained by God himself. So yes…much of the murder there was done in reverence of God. The stoning of women, the killing of firstborns, and on and on. But then Christ comes along and dies for mankind's sins. He is the final sacrifice of a loving God."

"I see," Mackenzie said, although she was still struggling with it. "And given that the killer is using crucifixion as a symbolic thing, I'm assuming he's more centered on the teachings of Christ that Old Testament law. Would you agree?"

"I would. I find it even more telling that he's not skewing the crucifixion. Usually when you see the cross of Christ depicted in hate crimes, they are inverted or upside down—almost like a mockery. But this guy is sticking to true New Testament form."

"Was there anyone else in the Bible who was crucified?"

"Well, it was a common punishment that the Romans carried out, but we only actually see one in great detail in the story of Christ. It might be worth pointing out that when the apostle Peter was crucified under Emperor Caesar, he asked to be crucified upside down because he did not see himself as worthy of being tortured and killed in the same way as Christ."

So maybe this guy is glorifying those he kills, Mackenzie thought. *Maybe he's showing them the same respect and reverence as Jesus Christ.*

"Another thing I wanted to ask you," Mackenzie said. "And I know it's a long shot, but certainly worth a try." She pulled out her cell phone and brought up a map of the DC area. On it, she had already previously marked the coordinates where each murder had taken place, highlighted by a small red marker.

"These are where all of the killings occurred," she said. "Can you look at them and tell me if there might be any sort of Biblical significance or pattern?"

Benjamin studied the map closely, pulling a pair of bifocals from his shirt pocket and placing them on his head. "The first murder was here, at Blessed Heart, correct?" he asked.

"Yes.   Father   Costas."
Benjamin traced the routes between the markers on the nap with his

finger. "There's certainly no obvious pattern here," he said. "However, if this man is pulling so hard from the narrative of Jesus, I can't help but wonder…"

With that, he gave the phone back to her and walked to one of the bookshelves. He scanned a few titles before selecting one and pulling it down. It was a paperback with some wear and tear on it, a thin volume that he brought back to the couch.

"There is this trail of sorts that many scholars and greedy tourist traps over in Israel refer to as the Jesus Trail," he said. He flipped through a few pages in the book, stopping at a point a little over halfway through. "Right here," he said, pointing to it.

"I'm sorry," she said. "I'm not exactly well-versed in religion or much of the Bible. Can you explain what I'm looking at?"

"Certainly. See, there's a stretch of land in Israel that is believed to be the main thoroughfare Jesus Christ traveled while teaching. The so-called Jesus Trail starts at Nazareth and ends at Capernaum. As you see here," he said, tapping at a map on the page he had turned to, "the Sea of Galilee borders a portion of it."

"And this trail is well known?"

"To some," Benjamin said. "People who do the Biblical tour of Israel often check it out. It's about forty miles long and is littered with a few important places in terms of the life of Jesus."

"So why does it end at Capernaum?" Mackenzie asked.

"There's a passage in the Book of Mark that says, *And when he returned to Capernaum after some days, it was reported that he was at home.* Based on scripture, many think that Capernaum was essentially a sort of home base for His teachings."

"And why are you showing me this?"

"Well, it's the only notable trail that we know of for certain that Jesus walked," he said. "And now that I'm seeing the Jesus Trail and the path that this killer seems to be on…"

He handed the book to Mackenzie, to allow her to judge for herself. She placed her cell phone map on the page opposite the Jesus Trail. She studied the Jesus Trail map first—a north-bound line that shifted slightly to the south as it stretched from Nazareth, past Cana and Arbel, coming to an end at Capernaum.

There were numerous points of interest along the Jesus Trail but only four murder sites along the killer's path: Blessed Heart, Cornerstone, Living Word, and St. Peter's. She used her GPS tracking to provide an accurate path between the points she had flagged on the map and was nearly knocked over by what she saw.

At the start of the Jesus Trail, there was an inverted U-shape along the path, connecting Nazareth to a town called Mashhad. On

127

her map of the murder sites, the route between Blessed Heart and Cornerstone matched the shape of the trail almost perfectly. Then, from Cornerstone to Living Word, there was a slight slant to the northeast—the same as the Jesus Trail between Cana and Lavi.

This is it, she thought as she followed the digital line between Living Word and St. Peter's. *Oh my God...*

And just as she had assumed, the somewhat jagged and crooked line that continued on the Jesus Trail headed in the same direction.

She double checked again before getting too excited, but she knew this was it before she was done.

Blessed Heart and Nazareth line up.

Cornerstone and Mashhad line up almost perfectly.

Living Word is a little off from Lavi, but not much.

St. Peter's lines up with Arbel—and the route even takes the exact same strange little jagged turn on both maps.

"This is it," she said. "It's too perfect to rule out. The killer is following this map."

Benjamin was continuing to look back and forth between the maps, nodding. "Yes, it certainly seems so."

She pinched and scrolled her phone map, enlarging the area. "So I just need to know what churches are beyond St. Peter's—within about a twelve-mile radius. Do you have a map or listing of that sort of thing?"

"Not a complete one, no..."

"Wait, never mind," she said. She pulled up the options menu on her map app and asked the program to show her listings for churches in the selected area.

Nine listings popped up. She carefully mimicked the last portion of the Jesus Trail route on her screen with her finger. When she came to the end of the imagined trail, she found her finger hovering over two churches.

"Would you agree that these two churches would serve as somewhere near the location of where Capernaum would be?" she asked.

"I'd say so," Benjamin said.

Mackenzie got to her feet, still holding the book. "Would you mind if I took this with me?" she asked.

"Not at all. And please...do let me know if I can be of any further help."

"I will. But you've already been more help than you know."

"I'll be praying for you, Agent White," Benjamin said as he escorted her out of the library.

"Thank you," she said, truly meaning it.

It was odd, but for perhaps the first time in her life, she was able to take some solace out of knowing that someone was actively praying for her.

She did her best to hold on to that peace as she headed back toward FBI headquarters.

CHAPTER TWENTY SEVEN

She tried calling McGrath on her way to headquarters, hoping to fill him in before she got there. She got his voicemail and didn't bother leaving him a message, as she'd likely see him within an hour or so. When she reached the building twenty minutes later, she parked in the visitors' lot rather than the garage, sure that she'd be headed back out within several minutes.

She rushed inside and headed for the elevators. The doors slid open and before she got on, she was surprised to see Harrison and Yardley stepping off.

"Agent White," Yardley said. "You look anxious. What's going on?"

"Is McGrath in his office?"

"No, he's back over at the Third District Station," Harrison said. "Ellington is with him, too."

She weighed her options and decided driving back out to the Third District would be a waste of time. "Can you two come up with me for a second?" she asked. "I think I'm on to something and I need all the bodies I can get."

They took the elevator up to her office, where she pulled up the same map she had on her phone, but this time on her laptop screen. She then laid out Benjamin Holland's book on the desk, opening it to the map of the Jesus Trail.

"What's this?" Harrison asked, studying the map.

"One second," Mackenzie said, pulling out her phone again. This time, she called Ellington instead of McGrath, feeling certain there was a better chance that Ellington would answer if he saw that it was her. She sent a FaceTime call request rather than a standard call, wanting to be able to show him the maps along with Yardley and Harrison.

As she had hoped, Ellington answered on the second ring. There was the usual second or so of hesitation and then the screen popped up. She smiled at the sight of his face as he smiled at her.

"Hey, that background behind you looks familiar," he joked. "You back at headquarters?"

"I am. Look...is McGrath nearby?"

"Yeah, he's in a meeting with one of the detectives. Need me to get him?"

"Yes, please. How are things going with Simmons?"

Ellington was on the move, heading to wherever McGrath was. He held the phone in a way that still allowed her to see his face, just from an angle.

"Things are getting shaky. The more we learn about him, the more McGrath is coming around to your side of things. Simmons is clearly not our guy. If I had to make a guess, he'll be released within a few hours. And hopefully recommended to a damned good shrink. Who the hell confesses to something like this just for attention?"

That was a whole separate conversation that had nothing to do with the current case. So Mackenzie let it go.

"Okay, he's in here," Ellington said. "Just a second."

Ellington lowered the phone, leaving Mackenzie, Harrison, and Yardley to listen to murmured conversation for several moments. After a bit more jostling around, Ellington's phone once again featured his face. She saw McGrath standing behind him. He looked tired and irritated—a version of McGrath that Mackenzie did not like at all.

"You got something?" McGrath asked, straight and to the point like always.

"Yes, I think I do. I spoke with Benjamin Holland and he and I figured out something. There's this thing called the Jesus Trail out in Israel. You ever heard of it?"

"No," McGrath said. "Please enlighten us."

Mackenzie did just that. She had Harrison hold her phone to make sure she was able to point out the exact similarities in the Jesus Trail and the path the killer seemed to be traveling down. She wasn't even halfway through it before she heard McGrath utter a hushed and rather awed: *"Holy shit."*

Given the situation, she found it a rather ironic curse.

"So what church is going to serve as Capernaum on his DC-oriented trail?" Yardley asked.

"There are two candidates," she said. "There's Monument Baptist and the District Church of God. They're close enough together that they could both be the next on his list. I highly recommend that we have someone stake out those locations. Maybe even have someone stationed outside of them until we get our killer."

"Damned good work, White," McGrath said.

131

She let the compliment sink in but didn't take the time to appreciate it. She could feel herself slipping into a groove, the kind of rhythm she usually felt when she was just beginning to really wrap her mind around a case.

"Okay, I'd like to speak with Ellington alone, please."

McGrath tolled his eyes on the screen. "Fine," he said. "Yardley and Harrison, meet me down here at Third District PD. I'm not sure where your next post is, but we need to figure it out."

Yardley and Harrison gave little nods of salutation had headed out. On her phone, Ellington's face came back into view. He looked happier than he had when he'd originally answered it five minutes ago.

"You need a partner?" he asked.

"If you're busy down there, stay. Maybe you *should* stay until they release Simmons. Someone needs to be the voice of reason."

"And where are you headed?" he asked.

"I've got one last hunch I want to check on," she said. "After speaking with a woman at that meeting in Alexandria, I'm starting to think that the murders aren't acts of revenge. I think it's a form of glorification."

"Come again?"

She explained to him about the preacher who had referred to himself as glorifying the young people he had abused—of those teens taking the place of Jesus. She then referred to the brief conversation she'd had about the theory with Benjamin Holland.

"And what's your hunch?" Ellington asked.

"I'm wondering if maybe the killer is someone who really looked up to these men that he has killed. He crucified them in the same manner as Christ. Some he respected more, perhaps; that's why the wound in the side wasn't present on all of them. I'm wondering if we're looking for some type of disgraced priest or preacher. Someone with that sort of reverence toward these men..."

"Yeah, that seems to work out," Ellington said. "Keep me posted."

"I will."

"At the risk of seeming small-minded, I have to ask: do you know if you'll be back at the apartment at any point tonight?"

She wanted to be frustrated at the question but she felt it, too. That spark of lust and joy that comes with the peaks of any relationship. They were on a peak now, a peak that seemed to be coasting along nicely. But it just so happened that they both had very demanding jobs that came first more often than not.

"I don't know. We'll see. If you get there before I do, keep the bed warm."

"Can do. Be safe out there."

She smiled, nodded, and ended the call. She then gathered up Benjamin Holland's book and headed right back out the door.

Outside, night was falling over DC. But Mackenzie had a funny feeling that her day was just getting started.

CHAPTER TWENTY EIGHT

Because of the high stakes of the investigation, Mackenzie was able to get the phone number she needed with just two simple requests. And although the phone number she was seeking was fairly high profile, it was handed to her almost flippantly. As she made the call to Auxiliary Bishop Whitter, the ease in getting his number made her realize just how much McGrath and the entire bureau were relying on her.

Whitter answered on the third ring and when Mackenzie introduced herself, he seemed absolutely livid.

"Agent White, I think I made it quite clear when we last spoke that I wanted nothing to do with you."

"Yes, sir. You did. And I—"

"Oh, you can stop right there," Whitter said. "You've been quite rude and insulting to my faith. Be advised that I will be contacting your supervisor and filing a formal complaint."

"That's great, actually," Mackenzie said. "Because he's the one who has given me full authority over this case. So if you call him to complain about me, be ready to answer some questions about obstructing information about the case."

"You're bluffing."

"Oh, I'm afraid not. If you want, I'll give you his name, number, and extension right now."

Whitter hesitated for a moment before finally responding. His voice was low and almost like the hiss of a snake. She could imagine him clenching his fist around his phone and speaking through his teeth on the other end.

"Fine. There's a coffee shop on Georgina Avenue. Cuppa Joe, it's called. You know it?"

"Coffee," she said dreamily. And then, because she felt like she was on a roll and simply could not help herself, she added: "Hallelujah!"

***

The good people of Washington, DC, liked their coffee, as was evidenced in the ridiculous line in the coffee shop. Mackenzie spotted Auxiliary Bishop Whitter right away, sitting in the back of the shop. Resisting the tempting scent of a brewing dark roast, Mackenzie headed to the back to meet him.

He looked pissed when she sat down across from him. She racked her brain, trying to figure out what she had done that might have upset him so badly the last time. Apparently the higher-ups in the Catholic Church did not appreciate having the dirt of their brethren thrown in their face in such a blatant way.

But Mackenzie had never been in the business of softening her words to save a few hurt feelings. Especially not now that she felt she was closing in on solid answers.

"I take it you're still at a loss on the current case?" Whitter asked.

"Actually, I've recently come across a promising theory," she said. "We're taking steps toward what we think is finalizing a plan. However, one can never have enough leads. Because of that, I was hoping to run something by you."

"More deplorable accusations?" Whitter asked, incredulous.

"No, actually. I am starting to believe that these murders are not murders of hatred or revenge. I believe the killer has a skewed sort of respect for the victims—that he is using the act of symbolism of crucifixion as a way to glorify his victims. He believes they deserve the same death and reverence as Jesus."

The thought seemed to land hard on Whitter. His anger slowly dissolved into something else. Sadness, maybe, or horror.

"We also believe the killer is mimicking the path of the so-called Jesus Trail, another indication that the killings are a show of respect rather than vengeance."

"I see," Whitter said, his attitude a bit softer now. "So how do you believe I can be of service to you this time around?"

"Well, the ample dedication and adoration from such a man leads me to believe that we're not talking about a regular person with a messed up theology. Someone this driven must know and love Christ intimately…albeit while also having some sort of mental imbalance."

"You think it's someone within the church?"

"I think it's a strong possibility."

"You don't think you might be trying to demonize men of the cloth in this little hunt?"

"With all due respect," Mackenzie said, "at this point in the investigation, things like jobs and religious preference isn't a factor. I don't care who he is, I don't care what he believes, and I really don't care where he chooses to worship. So no...I am not demonizing anyone. I'm simply trying to nail down a profile."

"So I ask again: how do you expect me to help?"

"I need to know if you can think of any priests—or preachers or pastors or whatever—in the area who have often been frowned upon because they might have been a little too overzealous. Maybe someone with a shady history that they were never really all that up front about?"

She could tell right away that Whitter had a name in mind. She could see it in the way his eyes instantly trailed away from her one second after she asked the question.

"You understand," he said, "that this is difficult for a man in my position. It is, to borrow a reference from the Bible, pointing out the splinter in my brother's eye when there is a plank in my own."

"Yes, but withholding information that might allow this killer to carry out another murder is only going to make that plank larger."

Whitter let out a shaky sigh and looked like he might actually break down in tears. Mackenzie could actually see the internal conflict working itself in the expressions that showed on his face.

"About five years ago," Whitter finally said, "there was a man named Joseph Hinkley. He came to DC from some place in Alabama. He was a Baptist who was absolutely on fire for the Lord. He had a post here in town at a very small church, and it only lasted a few months. He was one of these hellfire-and-brimstone preachers, wanting to get people saved by the fear of damnation rather than the love and promises of Christ. He took a lot of that Old Testament stuff seriously. Adulterers should be stoned, a woman has no place working or in the pulpit, things like that."

"You said he only lasted a few months with that church," Mackenzie said. "Was he released?"

"Yeah. Rumor has it he tried serving as an interim pastor at a few other churches. Honestly, I never paid it much mind. Catholics don't generally concern themselves with Baptists. However, he *did* place himself on my radar when he started approaching Catholic churches. He tried convincing a few—Blessed Heart was one, if I recall correctly—to allow him to speak here and there."

"I assume no one ever took him on?"

"Correct. Although word has it that he pops up at revivals every now and then. The kind where it's all under a tent and there's a lot of yelling and threatening the sin out of people. I suppose some say he's a former disgraced preacher. But the thing of it was...he seemed to be fascinated with not just Christ, but the men

136

who spoke about Him. He felt that the people that communicated the truth of Jesus to the masses deserved nearly the same acclaim as the messiah."

"And is that not common in religious circles?"

"No. It's blasphemous. And whenever someone comes close to behaving in such a way, they usually repent of it. But Joseph Hinkley used it as the crux of his message, from what I understand."

"Any idea where he lives, by any chance?" she asked.

"No. I do believe he's still around DC, though. I hear his name pop up from time to time. And not in any good ways."

"Thank you," Mackenzie said. "I know it pained you to speak with me again."

"I think I've explained myself well," he said. "I have no qualms with you—but I do resent a government and media that are forever angling my faith as a breeding ground for intolerance and hatred."

"That's the last thing I want to do."

·"And I believe that about you," Whitter said. "You've been in my prayers, Agent White. Despite the way it may seem, I truly do hope you are able to end this very quickly."

"Same here," Mackenzie said. And not sure how else to respond, she added: "And thanks for the prayers."

"Do you believe they work?" Whitter asked, as if surprised.

Mackenzie shrugged. "I don't know," she said, answering honestly. "But I know that *you* believe they do. And that in and of itself means a great deal to me."

With that, she gave him a nod of thanks and got to her feet. The line at the counter had gone down, so she joined it and read through the menu. She wasn't tired (and doubted she would be any time soon) but an extra jolt of caffeine never hurt.

She had the feeling it was going to be a long night.

She continued to roll it out by pulling out her phone and texting Harrison. **Joseph Hinkley,** she typed. **Former Baptist preacher. I need his info ASAP.**

CHAPTER TWENTY NINE

Harrison was as quick and effective as ever. By the time Mackenzie was back in her car and taking the first sip of her dark roast, he was calling. She savored the taste of the coffee for a moment before answering, hoping that Hinkley would prove to be another stepping stone—something as useful as the Jesus Trail information.

"You really know how to pick 'em, White," Harrison said.

"Tell me."

"Joseph Hinkley has basically no record to speak of until the age of thirty-seven. His first blip came seven years ago when he was arrested for assaulting a police officer in Baltimore while at a protest against a Muslim mosque being constructed. A year later, he was arrested for beating his wife, hitting her twice in the face and once in the ribs. After she left him, he shacked up with a twenty-two-year-old. He beat up on her, too. I'm looking at the records here and he apparently claims that he beat them because they did not appreciate the Lord and His ways and so he had to punish them."

"Anything worse than that?"

"Not from what I'm seeing. He's mentioned in a few cross-referenced cases where he was at the scene of protests or controversial events where there was a heavy police presence involved but no...no red flags otherwise."

"Got an address?" she asked.

"I do. I'll text it to you when we end the call."

Harrison was true to his word, delivering the text within ten seconds of Mackenzie ending their call. She was about to plug the address into her GPS but saw that she didn't need to. She was familiar with the location. She had, in fact, been very close to it less than four days ago.

As it turned out, Joseph Hinkley lived on Bedford Avenue—less than a mile away from Cornerstone Presbyterian.

***

Protocol deemed it necessary that, because Hinkley was a convicted wife beater, Mackenzie go with a partner. And because Ellington was still running the dead-end of Joseph Simmons, it was Harrison who tagged along with her. He seemed more than happy to be a part of it—perhaps for just a taste of what it had briefly been like to be her partner before his mother had passed away. Or maybe he was just tired of sitting behind a desk and being a glorified research hound.

Mackenzie was glad to have him. He was eager and enthusiastic. And from a professional point of view, she knew that he could use the practice.

When she and Harrison arrived at Hinkley's residence, there was no question that someone was home. In fact, quite a few people were home. Mackenzie counted four cars in the small driveway. It also seemed as if every light in the place was on. As she stepped out of her car and walked toward the porch, she saw two people walk directly by the front window, their backs to her.

"Some kind of little party or something?" Harrison asked.

"If that's the case," Mackenzie said, "it looks like a pretty lame party."

The house was nothing to write home about. It was a sloppy two-story that looked like it had been around awhile. Its age showed on the porch. The porch light revealed peeling and chipped paint along the façade and a front door that had fought its fair share of mildew.

The porch light was on, indicating that at least three of the cars in the driveway belonged to guests. She walked to the door and knocked, hearing the murmured voices of at last two people. There was a very slight commotion from inside as someone came to the door. It was answered by a man in his late forties, showing a wide smile between a bushy moustache and beard.

"Can I help you?" the man asked.

"Are you Joseph Hinkley?" she asked.

"I am. And you are?"

She showed her ID as she introduced herself. "I'm Agent Mackenzie White with the FBI." She nodded beside her and said, "And this is my partner, Agent Harrison. I was hoping you'd have the time to answer a few questions."

Hinkley looked alarmed and confused. He briefly looked over his shoulder for a moment before stepping into the doorway and pulling the door mostly closed behind him.

"What's this about?" he asked.

Mackenzie looked toward the crack in the door, gazing past the small swirl of nighttime insects that hovered by the porch light. "Do you have company tonight, Mr. Hinkley?" she asked.

"I do. It's a Bible study I do out of my home twice a week. Tonight is all about the book of Lamentations. Do you know it?"

She smirked at him and shook her head. "I wanted to ask *you* some questions, remember?"

"Yes," he said. "And yes...I can answer whatever questions you have. Would you care to come inside?"

"Yes, please."

He ushered the agents through the door and into the house's living room. There, five other men were sitting around a coffee table that held three Bibles. They had been in the midst of conversation until Mackenzie and Harrison stepped into the room.

"Sorry, men," Hinkley said. "Can you give me just a few minutes? Feel free to continue, though. Corey...pick up with Chapter Three, Verse Seven."

One of the men nodded as Hinkley led the agents down a small hallway and into the kitchen. Like the porch, the kitchen also showed the house's age. The linoleum was dingy and peeling slightly up at the corners. There was a suppressed smell of mildew and garbage—the smells of a man who didn't care much about the way people viewed his home.

"Can I offer you a soda or water?" Hinkley asked.

"No thank you," she and Harrison said, nearly in unison.

Hinkley shrugged. "It's the least I can do for a nice woman like yourself who is sent out into the dead of night to strange men's houses. Such a shame. Does the government not take such things into consideration?"

Wow, Mackenzie thought. *He really does have some old-school issues.*

"Honestly, I only have a few questions for you," Mackenzie said. "If all goes well, you'll be back to your study in five minutes or so."

"By all means, ask away," Hinkley said.

"Your name has come up in a case I'm working on. Between the two of us, it's a link that I'm not feeling is a strong one. But I have to look into everything."

She saw at once that her flippant attitude put him at ease. His guard was completely lowered now, making it much more likely that he'd reveal some small detail that might help her nail him...if he was the one to be nailed, of course.

"Is it about these poor murdered men of God?" he asked.

"It is. You've seen the stories on the news, I take it?"

"I have. And it's absolutely terrible."

"Did you know any of them personally?" Harrison asked.

"Not on any deep level, no."

"Given your history, did you ever cross paths with any of them?" Mackenzie asked.

"Well, I spoke with Reverend Tuttle quite often. As I'm sure you know, Cornerstone is right up the road from here. Some days—not too often, but often enough that it became something of a habit—I'd stop by there if I saw him petering around outside the place. He sometimes cut the grass and did the landscaping himself, you know."

"So you were on friendly terms when he died?"

"As far as I know. He and I disagreed on a lot of things in the Good Book but he was always very open-minded. He never spoke down to me or tried to change my mind. I liked him quite a bit."

"And what kind of things would he try to change your mind about?"

Hinkley grinned here; it was a sad sort of grin, one that seemed to very badly want to be a frown or a sneer instead. "As good of a man as he was, Reverend Tuttle was among the vast percentage of so-called followers of Christ that take the Old Testament as just some general suggestions. He softened the wrath of God into nothing but love."

"Is that so bad?" Mackenzie asked.

"For the world...no. But this is a fallen world. And it's fallen because Man decided to disobey God. When you take the wrath and strictness of God away, you have nothing but a fake set of guidelines. But like I said...I did not fault him and he did not fault me. We were always civil about our disagreements."

"Did you know any of the others?"

"Not well. I'd seen Pastor Woodall speak a few times. Once I went up at the end of service to ask for clarification on something. He was a smart man. Maybe too smart for his own good. He let intellect get in the way of his salvation, if you ask me. And Father Coyle...I spoke with him maybe a handful of times. I met him at a protest a few years back and we had a really good conversation."

"What sort of protest?"

"An anti-abortion rally," Hinkley said, rather proudly.

Don't even take that bait, Mackenzie told herself. She then realized that it wasn't bait. He was speaking as plain and as honestly as he could.

"Would you be able to provide your whereabouts for the last several nights?" Harrison asked.

Hinkley nodded solemnly, as if he had known the conversation was eventually coming to this. Without him saying a word to her, his expression told her that he knew she was eyeing him as a potential suspect.

"Off the top of my head, I can give you pretty specific details for every night up until about nine or ten days ago."

"That would be great," Mackenzie said.

"Well, I was in Virginia, down in the southeastern part, for three days last week. I've only been back in DC for four days."

"And what were you doing there?" she asked.

"I attended one revival and spoke at another one," he said. "If it helps, I've got the hotel receipts to prove it."

He's not lying, she thought. *If I asked him to fetch them, he would. He'd do it right now and I'd have them in my hand within two minutes. And he'd have a shit-eating grin on his face about it the entire time.*

"What about the last four nights?" she asked.

"I was here all of those nights. We had a Bible study three nights ago. It went on until ten or so."

Mackenzie was about to ask a follow-up question when her phone buzzed in her pocket. When she saw that it was Ellington, her thumb hovered over ANSWER.

"Mr. Hinkley, would you mind showing me those receipts?"

"Of course," he said. "One moment."

As Hinkley left the kitchen, Mackenzie looked to Harrison quickly. "Your initial thoughts?"

"He seems like a creep but I don't think he's our guy."

"Same here," Mackenzie said. "One second," she added, gesturing to her phone. She then answered the call with: "Hey. What's up?"

"I thought I'd let you know that the patrols in front of those churches isn't going to be as high of a priority as McGrath originally let on," Ellington said.

"And why not? Does he have a better idea?"

"Well, it's stretching manpower pretty thin. He may still have patrols outside of them, but it's not going to take priority."

"Isn't he the one who wanted this wrapped up quickly before everyone on the Hill came crashing down on him? But he's worried about manpower?"

"Think about it, Mac. What's going to be more effective? A few agents actively out hunting for this guy or a few agents sitting still, hoping that the killer *might* just show up. Besides…he killed last night. The other murders have been spaced out. The odds that he'd strike tonight are slim to none. We can't just sit and wait."

He's right, she thought. But still, she felt that it was a mistake. The Jesus Trail lead seemed solid and she felt that there *had* to be pay dirt at the end of it.

"Okay," she said. "Thanks for letting me know."

She ended the call as she saw Hinkley already coming back down the hallway toward the kitchen. When he handed her the receipts, he did so with a crooked smile on his face. *Here's the proof of how absolutely wrong you are,* that smile seemed to say.

She looked the receipts over and saw that they were legit. Harrison was looking over her shoulder at them, too, giving them an eye of scrutiny. Mackenzie knew that she could call the motel and make sure he had not checked in and then left just to come back to DC to enact his killings. But that was a long shot and it felt desperate.

It's not him, she thought. *You knew that a few minutes ago, from the way he spoke about Tuttle. So let it go and move on.*

"Thank you for your cooperation," she said, handing him the receipts. "I'll let you get back to your Bible study now."

"Thanks. And Agent…it's sort of sad, isn't it?"

"What is?"

"The fact that men who claim to believe so fervently in God would find someone who disagreed with them so alarming that they point fingers. It makes them feel comfortable. It makes it easier for them to turn their backs on their own sin."

Like the splinter and the plank Whitter mentioned, Mackenzie thought…not without a hint of irony.

"Sorry if that upsets you," Hinkley said

No you're not, she thought.

"Agent Harrison," Hinkley said, "please make sure you are always looking out for Agent White. Her outfit is tight-fitting, the skirt too high. And we live in evil times after all."

"With all due respect," Harrison said, "Agent White needs no protection."

Mackenzie said nothing, though she did smile. She also offered a simple nod to Hinkley as she made her way back down the hall with Harrison following behind. She didn't even so much as bother to look back into the small group of men huddled in the living room for the study. She walked directly back out into the night and increased her speed as she walked toward her car. She was rather glad that Harrison was with her. The mere fact that someone else was there with her helped her to stay grounded, not letting her discouragement get the better of her.

Even if he *was* innocent, Hinkley had unnerved her a bit. There was a certainty to him—an absolute assurance that he was right and the men who had been killed were all wrong. And if that was the case, then he surely would not have killed those men with glorification as a motive.

Maybe we got the glorification thing wrong, she thought. *And if that's the case, what else did we get wrong?*

It was a troubling thought, and one that had her nearly peeling rubber out of Joseph Hinkley's driveway.

CHAPTER THIRTY

Although it required some extra driving, Mackenzie left Hinkley's residence and drove out to Monument Baptist and the District Church of God. Monument Baptist came first. The two were so close that when she stepped out of her car and onto the sidewalk, she could literally see the steeple rising in a shadow-shape of the night further up the street and on the other side.

She also saw that there was a decoy car parked in front of Monument Baptist, the sort of featureless 2005 model that was usually parked in the bureau parking garage. She raised her hand to the man inside, a gesture of acknowledgment. The figure inside returned it, the movement tired and listless.

Poor guys is bored out of his mind, Mackenzie thought. *Maybe he wouldn't be if this site was given the attention it should.*

The night was dark—only a quarter of the moon was visible—so she used her flashlight to check the grounds. Monument Baptist was quite small, roughly as small as the tiny church she had met Benjamin Holland in. There was a small graveyard on the back of the property, something she rarely saw in the city, and it added a creepy quality to the whole scene. After a circuit of the property, she drove farther up the block to the District Church of God.

This church looked almost like a small store. A blacktop parking lot was perfectly trimmed out front. When she walked up to the large picture windows that looked in, she could see very little with her flashlight.

Maybe Ellington and McGrath are right, she thought. *More than one or two people stationed here might be a waste. The other churches had a sense of charm and beauty to them—even the much tinier Cornerstone Presbyterian. These two places...they're like old forgotten monuments to a God people only kinda-sorta believe in.*

Unsure of whether or not her encounter with Hinkley was simply making her feel defeated, Mackenzie knew that she needed to get back behind the files. She needed to be comfortable, her mind devoid of anything. Even if she *was* wrong about these two churches, she still felt like she was on to *something*.

But what?

It was a good question. And it was a question she intended to have an answer to before the sun came up. She went back to her car, waving at the man on patrol again as she passed. This time, he barely even raised his hand back to her.

***

Ellington was already home when she got there. And although he was getting ready for bed and made jokes about how they could *both* get the bed warm, she passed. She *had* to get to those files. Fortunately, Ellington knew all about her work ethic and did not take it personally. He also did not offer to help, knowing full well that she would turn him down there as well.

And he did not complain about any of it. He simply knew her *that* well, knowing that she had to work alone, in perfect quiet and with no distractions.

That's why I love him, she thought. *That's why, if I get my way, I'm going to end up marrying him.*

She pulled a soda from the fridge at 11:15 p.m. and started looking over the case files again. Crime scene photos. Forensics reports. Everything she could find from her physical files and in all of the emails and digital documents she had on her computer.

She saw the same thing in all of the photos. All of the men had been killed, stripped mostly naked, and crucified in a manner that depicted Christ.

But even if these are acts of glorification, it's being done by a killer, she thought. *And for someone who has no qualms about killing, something as seemingly simple as glory would be skewed.*

She looked at the pictures side by side. Each murder...something was different at each one. There was just enough to indicate a purpose behind it. There was the faint cut in the side on Woodall, then the nastier, very clear gash in Coyle's side. Also, with Coyle, there had been the personal items at the foot of the cross.

It's like he's building to something. And he's taking his sweet time about it.

As gruesome as it seemed, she doubted that one more murder would satisfy this guy. So if they were to work on the assumption that the Jesus Trail approach was right, maybe there was more than one more stop along the way—the equivalent of Capernaum.

Or what if there's a different course? Was there maybe some other well-known route that Jesus walked?

146

She spent some time on Google and came up with nothing. The Jesus Trail kept popping up over and over again.

By the time she was on her second soda, Mackenzie had resorted to digging up information on all four of the deceased. She saw a few articles on them, and Father Costas even had a Wikipedia page. On the page, there was a picture of him speaking from the pulpit, a fatherly smile on his face. His elegant church was behind him—the white colors, the ornate but tasteful columns, a strange but tranquil embossed piece of art.

A few minutes later she came across a YouTube video of Pastor Woodall. He was giving a tour of his church. The tour was co-led by a man Mackenzie had met on the morning Woodall had been killed—Dave Wylerman, the music director. As the video led the viewer through the sanctuary (a large room that looked more like a theater than a church), Mackenzie noted the differences between the interiors of Living Word and Blessed Heart. Where Blessed Heart was bright, highlighted in faux golds and natural light spilling in everywhere, it seemed that Living Word was more about mute colors and earth tones. Even the paintings on the wall of Living Word's large entry room seemed to be dark and muted.

She almost missed it because it was so unappealing. But after a moment of hesitation, she stopped the video and backed it up ten seconds. She watched as Woodall and Wylerman walked through the entry room and then paused the video when the painting came back into view.

She studied it for a moment and shrunk the window size. She then opened up the Wikipedia page for Father Costas again and shrunk that one as well. She zoomed in a bit on his picture and then slid the windows side by side.

The painting in the background of Living Word bore a few similarities to the embossed art behind Father Costas in his picture.

Curious now, she sent a text to Harrison. She knew he was a night owl and that he'd likely respond as quickly as usual. **Do we have ANY pictures of the interiors of Cornerstone or St. Peter's?**

While she waited, she ran a Google image search for *Cornerstone Presbyterian, Washington, DC.* She had to scroll for a bit until she found anything but even then, it was not much. A few pictures of a cookout for the Vacation Bible School last year. A picture of a visiting choir. A few images of Reverend Tuttle. Nothing else.

She received a text back from Harrison eleven minutes after she had sent it. Slow for Harrison, but not too bad considering it had somehow come to be 1:48 in the morning.

Had to forward the request to records, he replied. **Case is sensitive, so they hopped on it. They're sending you a mail with some interior shots of St. Peters from after Coyle's murder.**

She checked her email and sure enough, there was an email from Records waiting for her. It was titled *St. Peter's.*

She opened the mail and clicked the link inside of it. She was directed to a bureau file sharing service where there were eighteen pictures of the interior of St. Peter's. She didn't make it past the second one before she saw what she was looking for.

In the background, behind the sanctuary and damn near centered perfectly in the picture, was a piece of faux relief artwork. While it did not appear to be the same style as what she had haphazardly seen in Living Word or Blessed Heart, there were many similarities.

It was far too much to ignore.

In fact, in that moment, it seemed incredibly important.

She looked at the clock and then at her phone. 2:03 in the morning.

She had no choice. Sure that the poor man would soon come to hate her very much, Mackenzie placed a call to Benjamin Holland.

CHAPTER THIRTY ONE

Mackenzie was surprised and relieved to see that Benjamin did not look nearly as tired as she had expected him to be. It was 2:50 when she followed him back into the small library in the back of the small church. He seemed almost happy to be there, as if he might be returning to his favorite place in the world.

"I can't tell you how much I appreciate you meeting me at such a miserable hour," Mackenzie said.

Benjamin shrugged as she plopped down in the couch. "I'm a bit of a night owl anyway," he said. "I was just getting ready to settle down for the night when you called."

"I'll try to see to it that you return to your bed as soon as possible," she said.

She was wearing her laptop bag over her shoulder. She slid it off, opened up her laptop, and pulled up the images she had been studying so hard in her apartment.

"While we are still strongly considering the Jesus Trail approach, there is something else I noticed in some of these images. At first I thought it might be nothing, but I don't know…it seems a little too coincidental to me."

"Well," Benjamin said. "Let's see what you have."

Mackenzie spent the next few moments walking him through how she had come to find the images—of the piece of art behind Father Costas, the painting in Living Word, the faux relief art at St. Peter's. They then studied the images closely. Benjamin seemed rather fascinated as he studied the pictures, a smile forming at the corners of his mouth.

"Do you recognize the artwork?" she asked.

"I do," he said. "I mean, I've never actually been in St. Peter's before so I have not actually *seen* that artwork, but I *do* recognize it for what it is. All three of these pictures you've stumbled across…they are three stages of the Stations of the Cross."

"What's that, exactly?" she asked, again not liking the feeling of being uneducated in any specific area.

"In Latin, it's referred to as *Via Crucis*. It's depictions of what Christ went through on the day he was crucified. There are fourteen of them—fourteen images that show several scenes from that day. It

149

starts at the moment that Pilate condemned Christ to die and ends when he is placed in a tomb. There's a somewhat unofficial fifteenth depiction showing Christ being resurrected."

"And this is a well-known thing?"

"Not really," he said. As if struck by an afterthought, Benjamin got up from the couch and started to look through the titles. He ran his finger expertly along the spines, looking for a particular one.

"If you yank some random person in off of the street and ask them about it, they'll likely have no idea what you're talking about," he continued. "I suppose, though, if you live in Jerusalem, you'd know about it. There's an alleyway in the city known as the Via Dolorosa that has these stations numbered. People can travel down it as a form of remembrance and prayer. Of course, as we see in these pictures, there are replicated depictions all throughout the world. One of the more popular, I believe, is located in Portugal."

That said, he selected a book from the shelf and started thumbing through it as he walked back to the couch. By the time he got back to the couch, he had found the place he was looking for and handed the book over to Mackenzie.

She looked at the pages in front of her and saw a few different depictions of scenes from the Stations of the Cross. There was a gorgeous one in Portugal at the Shrine of Our Lady of Fatima. There was an entire colorful set located in the Portuguese church at Kolkata. As she flipped to the next page, she even saw pictures showing people reenacting Christ's walk to Golgotha, complete with huge crosses strapped to the backs of the actors.

"Okay," Mackenzie said, feeling the pieces fall into place. "So what can you tell me about the depictions from these churches here in DC?"

"Well, the one we see from Living Word is pretty clear, I think. It shows Christ falling from the weight of the cross on his back. Now, during the Stations, he falls three times but each time he falls, there are more people around him, depicting the gathering crowds come to watch him die. Given that there are very few onlookers in this depiction, I'd say this is the first time he fell."

"Of the fourteen stations, where does this one fall in order?"

Benjamin took the book from her, flipped a few pages, and came to a page that listed out the order of the Stations. "Here," he said. "That would be the third station."

"And the St. Peter's depiction?"

They both looked at the picture of the interior of St. Peter's. It showed a woman, presumably Mary, coming to the side of Christ as he continued on with his cross.

"Jesus meets Mary," Benjamin said. "That's the fourth station."

Another huge piece of the puzzle fell into place for Mackenzie. *If the Station of the Cross depiction in Blessed Heart represents the first station, I've got this bastard.*

Because the third station was in Living Word…and Pastor Woodall had been the third victim. And the fourth station was depicted in St. Peter's, and Father Coyle had been the fourth victim.

Another certainty arose in her, one that made her feel more certain than ever that this was the key.

This guy could easily kill his victims in their homes. But he is electing to do it at the churches. For some reason, he feels that it needs to take place at the location where that particular station is represented. All of these deaths…wherever the murders may take place, it all ends up at a church…

Together, Mackenzie and Benjamin looked at the image in Blessed Heart. She zoomed in on the station depiction behind Father Costas. She saw Christ, standing with a few other people while another small group stood over him on some sort of large stairway or stage of some kind. The man in the center looked quite regal and authoritarian. The certainty of it fell on Mackenzie at the same time Benjamin spoke it.

"That's the moment when Pilate condemned Christ to die," he said. "That's station one."

"He's going in order then," Mackenzie said.

"It would seem that way," Benjamin said gravely.

Mackenzie looked to the chronological listing of the stations. The fifth station relayed the scene of Simon coming to the aid of Christ to help him carry the cross.

"By any chance, do you know of any churches in DC that have artwork that represents the fifth station?" she asked.

"I'm afraid not," he said. "But I can make a few calls and see if we can get an answer."

"That would be extraordinary," she said.

"It might take a while, given the hour."

Mackenzie nodded, refusing to get discouraged again. "That's fine," she said. "Anything you can do to help would be greatly appreciated. Can you please call me the moment you get an answer?"

"*If* I get an answer, sure."

"I'll see what the bureau can do to also help get an answer," she said. "Thanks again."

With that, she left the study for the second time in less than twelve hours.

151

This is it, she thought. *This is the connection. This is what is going to help us nail this asshole.*

She ran to her car and nearly peeled out of the parking spot as she headed toward FBI headquarters.

CHAPTER THIRTY TWO

Mackenzie had not been sure how long it would take to find a piece of random information as bizarre and out of the blue as what she and Benjamin were looking for. Still, when 4:30 rolled around and she found herself standing in a conference room with three other agents and no further answers, she started to feel as if time was slipping away from them. It reached the point where she was expecting the phone to ring at any moment—either with good news from Benjamin, or with terrible news that the killer had struck again while they were busy making phone calls to churches to ask about the art they had hanging in their halls and sanctuaries.

Ellington, Yardley, and Harrison were all in the room with her. Yardley was checking all art museum donation records from the past fifty years, looking for any indication that a depiction of the fifth Station of the Cross had been given to a local church. Harrison was apologetically calling the leaders of every church he could get the contact information for, asking about the artwork in their church. Ellington was running interference and trying to keep McGrath happy, doing what he could to properly explain Mackenzie's discovery pertaining to the Stations.

Mackenzie, meanwhile, was continuing to research the Stations and their significance to different denominations. Maybe she could find motive buried somewhere in the history and theology of it all. She almost wished she was back in Benjamin Holland's study, around his seemingly unlimited resource of religious texts. Instead, she settled for what she had: Google and Wikipedia.

Ellington, having been on the phone with McGrath for the past several minutes, put his cell phone down and took a seat next to Mackenzie.

"So, he's not too happy," he said.

"Of course he's not. I haven't offered some magic trick to point a finger directly at the killer."

"Well, yeah, there's that," Ellington said. "But he'd still pissed about you wanting to stake out those two churches—which, by the way, he *is* doing. There are cars going by once every hour or so."

"So I guess he's upset that the four of us are huddled up in this conference room, trying to pin down this church?"

"Yeah, he's not too happy about that. He said he'll be back by here in about an hour or so. He's busy with something else right now."

"Did he say what?"

Ellington shook his head. "No. Whatever it is, he's holding this one pretty close to his belt."

"I don't see what—" she started to say, but her phone interrupted her.

She answered it right away, recognizing the number.

It was Benjamin Holland.

"Please tell me you got it," she said.

"I do. A friend of mine in Belgium is an avid collector of religious art and keeps up with this sort of thing. He actually had a list of all American churches with any sort of depictions of the Stations of the Cross. He has three listings for churches in DC that have depictions of the fifth station. One of those churches has closed in the last few years, though, so that knocks your options down to two."

"That's great," she said.

"It gets better. Of those two churches, one of them dedicated their depiction to a museum for religious art somewhere in Mexico last year. So that leaves you only *one* church. Grace Baptist, over on Hudson Street."

"You're sure of this?" she asked.

"I am. I had him confirm it. I'll text you the phone number over there. I don't have the number for anyone on leadership, though."

"That's okay. This is perfect. Thanks, Benjamin."

She hung up before he could get out his entire response of *You're welcome.*

"Got it," she announced to the room, pulling up McGrath's number.

"Got what?" Harrison asked. "The church?"

"Yes. Benjamin Holland came through in a big way."

"Are you calling McGrath?" Ellington asked. After she nodded, Ellington winced. "I don't know if that's the best idea."

But it was too late. The phone had rung twice and McGrath answered in his usual curt manner.

"What is it, White?"

"Grace Baptist," she said. "That's where the fifth Station of the Cross is located."

"You're certain of this?"

"Yes. It's information that came directly from a close friend of Benjamin Holland. Ellington and I will head over there now and—"

154

"No. I don't want our manpower spread so thin over this. It's already pretty damned thin as it is. You head over there and if it seems like it pans out, *then* you call. If you know for certain there's anything to it, call and I'll send every available agent."

"Sir, what's going on?"

"I'm just swamped, White. I'm up to my eyeballs in other shit. The world does not revolve around your case."

"It sounded like it did the last time we spoke," she said. She then snapped her mouth closed, realizing that she was smarting off to McGrath. And that could do nothing other than complicate matters even worse.

"I'm going to pretend the last five seconds never happened, so consider that a warning to your smart mouth," he said. "Now, if you feel that this is a solid lead, please go check it out. If it comes to anything, call for whatever help you need."

He ended the call abruptly, leaving Mackenzie with a silent phone in her hands. She stared at it, dumbfounded.

"That bad, huh?" Ellington asked.

She sighed and pocketed her phone. "I'm going to head over there and check it out. If it comes to anything, I'll call. Be on standby, all of you?"

Yardley and Harrison nodded, Yardley with a look of apprehension on her face. Ellington, meanwhile, walked her out the door and when they were alone, he took her hands.

"You okay?" he asked.

"Yeah. McGrath is being...I don't know. He's hiding something."

"I gathered that, too. I'll see what I can find out. In the meantime, you be careful. And give me a call if you so much as *smell* trouble."

She nodded and leaned in to kiss him. It was sweet and lingering, just the thing she needed to send an extra little jolt of energy into her. With the kiss having supplied a bit more energy, it was easy to ignore the fact that she had not slept last night.

Wide awake and with a promising lead ahead of her, she headed back down to her car as the night started to fade away in the wake of the approaching morning.

CHAPTER THIRTY THREE

Coming to a stop at a stoplight, Mackenzie pulled out her phone and typed **Grace Baptist** into Google. The page came up and it only took her a few moments to find the About Us page. There, she found the name of the lead pastor: Tim Armstrong. There was no personal contact number, just the church's number followed by an extension.

She sent a group text to Ellington, Yardley, and Harrison. **I need the number for Tim Armstrong, lead pastor at Grace Baptist.**

In front of her, the light turned green and she took off. Her guts were churning, her heart hammering—her instinct telling her that she was on to something. The previous stoplight, she decided, would be the last she stopped for.

Then, for the third time, she tried the number Benjamin Holland had given her. It had only directed her to a recording from the church's welcome center the previous two times and it did the same this time as well. She was invited to punch in an extension or leave a message. She did neither; she figured if nothing happened between now and business hours starting up, she'd speak to someone face-to-face and make sure the church was under constant surveillance. The lead pastor may also need an escort. Of course, that might make finding the killer a bit harder, but—

You're getting too far ahead of yourself, she thought as she slowed to turn into the parking lot.

The sun was just beginning to deposit a few golden hues along the horizon when Mackenzie pulled her car into the lot of Grace Baptist. The church reminded her a bit of Living Word. It was big but not overly so. It was also designed in a rather modern feel, nothing like the Baptist churches Mackenzie had grown up around.

She looked to the right and saw only one car in the sizeable parking lot. Nothing about it sent alarm bells off, but it did make her think of one thing she had neglected to do before leaving headquarters.

She walked up to the church in the fading darkness of early dawn. Like Living Word, it had large picture windows that allowed her to look inside. As she expected, there was no one inside. She tried the double glass doors and, unsurprisingly, found them locked.

In her pocket, her cell phone buzzed at her. She removed it and saw that Yardley had texted back with Tim Armstrong's cell phone number. She tapped the number and the phone made the call for her right away. It rang five times and then went straight it voicemail. She didn't bother with a message, knowing that more than fifty percent of the time, it did no good. People tended not to even check their voicemail unless they were expecting an important call.

She knew it was far too early for most people—just now inching past 5:30 in the morning—but she figured this was an emergency. Also, while it might be a bit stereotypical, she was pretty sure any religious leader would be up early for prayer and quiet time. Apparently not Tim Armstrong, though.

Beginning to understand why McGrath may have thought she was being far too pushy about sending as much manpower as possible out here, Mackenzie started to walk around the building. She guessed that the building itself was roughly the length and width of a football field—probably shy by a few feet, but close. So trekking around it was not any small feat.

As she rounded a corner to the back of the church, she saw a small maintenance and tool shed sitting off to the edge of the property. Behind it was a wrought-iron fence that separated the church property from a neighboring property—the entrance to a well-to-do subdivision.

A sizeable stretch of lawn sat in the back of the church. A small playground was tucked away in the corner of the lawn, again separated from the neighboring property by the iron fence. A staff parking lot sat to the other side, completely empty.

Still feeling a sense of unease, she figured she'd try Armstrong's cell number again. Maybe if the same number called repeatedly, he'd be inclined to answer.

The phone started to ring in her ear. After the first ring, the sound was odd. It almost sounded as if it was echoing in her ear, like it was…

Like the phone is here, on the church grounds.

She removed the phone from her ear and listened closely. There it was again—the ringing of a cell phone. Without the phone to her ear, it was much easier to hear, much easier to trace.

It was coming from behind her. From the maintenance shed.

She returned her phone to her pocket and, without even thinking, unholstered her Glock.

Calm down, a small part of her said. *He could just be out here to check on supplies. Maybe gassing up the mower for later today.*

The wiser part of her recalled seeing the single car out in the parking lot. *At 5:30 in the morning,* this part of her argued.

She made her way quickly along the back patch of grass heading for the maintenance shed. It was a nicer model, one that had likely been purchased from the front lot of a Home Depot rather than built by hand. A large barn-style door was latched closed at the front. A single window was placed in the right side, reflecting the small bit of sunlight that had graced this side of the world.

She slowed her pace as she neared the shed. Rather than heading directly for the door, she went to the right side of the structure. She inched toward the window, the Glock held tightly in her hands. She turned toward the window quickly, looking in as stealthily as she could.

She saw the large planks on the floor first—one lay vertically, taking up almost the entire length of the shed. The other was horizontal, a little crooked and not quite across, but the idea was certainly there.

And then she saw the man.

He was stripped down to his underwear.

His right arm was stretched out awkwardly as he grabbed the horizontal plank.

No, she thought. *He's not grabbing it.*

The glare from the window made it hard to see it clearly, but his hand had been nailed to the plank. She could see the dark circle of blood within his palm as he struggled against the pain and weight.

She looked to his face as her stomach dropped. There was a gag tied around his head. His hair was gray and the frantic and pain-filled eyes she saw through the window had looked much happier and more peaceful when she had seen them in the photograph on the Grace Baptist website.

It was Tim Armstrong.

Mackenzie turned away from the window and headed for the shed's door.

When another man stepped around from the corner, she was too surprised at first to act as quickly as she usually did.

He was only one foot away from her when he drew a hammer up over his head. It was coming down, aimed for her skull, when she tried to sidestep and pull the trigger on her Glock at the same time.

The sound of her gunshot and the sickening *thump* of the hammer striking the side of her face filled the world at the same time.

Mackenzie's legs felt as if the bones had turned to jelly. She hit her knees, trying to raise her gun only to find that there was nothing in front of her eyes but darkness.

***

When she opened her eyes, the first thing she realized was that she could not breathe. The world was not dark, but tinted in a strange beige color. Her shoulders ached and her ankles stung. More than anything, though, her head hurt like hell.

Calm down, she thought. *Take inventory. What happened?*

She put the pieces together and as she did, was able to breathe again—and to get a better gauge on her situation.

Tim Armstrong was in the shed. One hand nailed to a cross that had not yet been constructed. A man came from around the corner and hit me with a hammer. But I got a shot off. Did I get him? Is he dead?

Given her current predicament, she assumed not.

As her sight started to come back—still beige-colored and blurry for now, but operable—she got a better idea of what was happening.

She was in the shed. Her hands were tied behind her back. Her ankles were bound. She was pushed into a corner, behind a riding lawn mower and a canister of gasoline.

She moved her head slowly. She looked to the window and saw that it was still murky outside. The sun had not yet risen.

So I haven't been blacked out for long. Maybe he just barely got me with that hammer.

This, too, was wishful thinking. Her head felt like a bomb had gone off in her skull. She could feel it swelling even without the use of her hands.

From her right, she could hear a clinking sound. This was followed by a murmur of desperation and a soft shuffling noise.

"Be still," a voice said. "It will be over soon. You are dying like Jesus. You, too, will be glorified."

Mackenzie couldn't see what was happening because the mower was blocking her line of sight. She fought against whatever was binding her wrists, but to little effect. They were tied tightly together. All the wrestling accomplished was cutting the side of her wrist on the edge of the riding mower's grass guard.

159

The pain and instant blood spilled from her skin was a godsend, though. An idea entered her mind that seemed both desperate and logical all at once. Again moving as quietly as she could, Mackenzie shifted her body to the right. She had to twist her shoulders awkwardly but she managed to align the tight binding around her wrists with the mower guard. She raised her arms and lowered them, up and down up and down, as quietly as she could.

She had no idea if it was working—if the guard was cutting through whatever had her wrists bound. She could tell that it was not anything steel or metal...it was maybe rope or some sort of heavy-duty cloth, or—

The garage was then filled with the heavy sound of a hammer striking a nail. A guttural cry of agony, muffled yet unmistakable, followed it. Mackenzie cringed at the noise but also used it to her advantage, taking the two or three seconds to intensify her awkward sawing motions.

She started to feel the pressure around her wrists loosen. She looked down at her ankles and saw that they had been tied with some sort of thick twine. If it was the same material that was holding her wrists together, she assumed she'd be able to saw through it fairly easily.

The murmured pain of Tim Armstrong became a gasping sort of wheezing. The scurried commotion of him writhing against the floor had come to a stop.

I'm going to hear him die if I don't hurry up, she thought.

Again, she heard the clinking of nails and then a clatter as a hammer was dropped to the floor.

"I know it hurts," the man said to Armstrong. "But it will be over soon. Lean on those everlasting arms until then. He's waiting for you, Pastor. He's waiting for you and you'll rejoice in his presence."

He is doing it as a form of glorification, she thought as she continued to saw. *He thinks he's doing them a favor—thinks he's delivering them to Christ.*

Two more slow and purposeful motions of her shoulders and she felt her wrists come completely free. Rather than leap up right away, she took a moment to flex her hands and stretch her wrists. She then quickly reached down and untied the twine around her ankles. It came off easily enough and when she was finally free, she got into a crouching position.

No gun, she thought. *A head that feels like it's cracked down the center and vision that's still not one hundred percent. Not the best odds.*

160

Blake Pierce

Blake Pierce is author of the bestselling RILEY PAGE mystery series, which includes eleven books (and counting). Blake Pierce is also the author of the MACKENZIE WHITE mystery series, comprising eight books (and counting); of the AVERY BLACK mystery series, comprising five books; and of the new KERI LOCKE mystery series, comprising five books (and counting).

An avid reader and lifelong fan of the mystery and thriller genres, Blake loves to hear from you, so please feel free to visit www.blakepierceauthor.com to learn more and stay in touch.

BOOKS BY BLAKE PIERCE

RILEY PAIGE MYSTERY SERIES
ONCE GONE (Book #1)
ONCE TAKEN (Book #2)
ONCE CRAVED (Book #3)
ONCE LURED (Book #4)
ONCE HUNTED (Book #5)
ONCE PINED (Book #6)
ONCE FORSAKEN (Book #7)
ONCE COLD (Book #8)
ONCE STALKED (Book #9)
ONCE LOST (Book #10)
ONCE BURIED (Book #11)

MACKENZIE WHITE MYSTERY SERIES
BEFORE HE KILLS (Book #1)
BEFORE HE SEES (Book #2)
BEFORE HE COVETS (Book #3)
BEFORE HE TAKES (Book #4)
BEFORE HE NEEDS (Book #5)
BEFORE HE FEELS (Book #6)
BEFORE HE SINS (Book #7)
BEFORE HE HUNTS (Book #8)

AVERY BLACK MYSTERY SERIES
CAUSE TO KILL (Book #1)
CAUSE TO RUN (Book #2)
CAUSE TO HIDE (Book #3)
CAUSE TO FEAR (Book #4)
CAUSE TO SAVE (Book #5)

KERI LOCKE MYSTERY SERIES
A TRACE OF DEATH (Book #1)
A TRACE OF MUDER (Book #2)
A TRACE OF VICE (Book #3)
A TRACE OF CRIME (Book #4)
A TRACE OF HOPE (Book #5)